MW00834080

SOLACE
ARISEN

*To Jennifer —
With all my appreciation!
Anna*

SOLACE ARISEN

SOLACE BOOK III

ANNA STEFFL

evenSO Press
Prairie Village, Kansas

Library of Congress Control Number: 2013958466

ISBN: 978-0-9911587-3-7

Printed in the United States of America

First Edition.

Cover Design and Interior format by The Killion Group
http://thekilliongroupinc.com

DEDICATION

To JMS and JEK

Solacians

Superior Madra Cassandra—head of the Solacian order

Hera Arvana Nazar (Hera Solace)—tasked with finding a champion to wield the Blue Eye

Hera Musette—spiritual advisor to Lady Martise in Acadia

Heran Kieran—a Solacian brother

Sarapostans

Prince Gregory Fassal—heir of Sarapost

Captain Myronan Degarius—leader of the Frontiersmen who carries Assaea, a blessed sword

Sergeant Jamis Micah

Corporal Salim

Corporal Nat

Chancellor Degarius—Degarius's father

Lina—Degarius's deceased grandmother

Stellan—Degarius's deceased grandfather

Acadians
King Dontyre Lerouge

Prince Chane Lerouge—by inheritance carries Artell, a blessed sword

Princess Jesquin Lerouge—Hera Arvana's student

Lady Martise—widow of the king's brother, hostess to Solacians in Acadia

Attaché Honor Keithan—assistant to the prince

Lord Sebastion—an impoverished nobleman

Miss Gallivere—a friend of the princess

Gherians

Sovereign Alenius

Breena—the sovereign's beloved

General Sibelian Aleniusson—adopted son of the sovereign

Cleric Nils—the sovereign's former advisor

Cleric Rorke—chief cleric of the Worship Hall

Captain Juvenot—keeper of Seraph

The asher—a newly made eunuch

Captain Berlson—of the Fortress Guard

Creatures

The Scyon—a spirit recalled from Hell

Seraph—the poison draeden

Megreth—the fire draeden

Ancient Heroes

Lukis—ended Reckoning with the blessed sword Artell

Paulus—ended Reckoning with the Blue Eye and the sword Assaea

Mariel—founder of Solace

Relics

Assaea—a blessed sword thought lost

Artell—a blessed sword kept by the Acadians

The Beckoner—a device that resurrects dead spirits into a new body

The Blue Eye—a device that can kill by drawing souls into Hell

The Easternland

YOU, IN WHOM ALL IS POSSIBLE

Solace

Pale light crept into the bottoms of the gathering room's east windows and into Superior Madra Cassandra's consciousness. It would be a fine day for travel. In a moment of amused reflection before calling the sisters sitting behind her from their meditation, she noted that the high windows were designed to let in light but not the distractions of the courtyard outside. They did little, however, to deter inward distractions. But today, perhaps, it was allowable to be distracted. Last night was Princess Lerouge's Coming of Age Ceremony and today Musette and Arvana would be coming home. The duty with the relic was over. Hera Arvana's letter, announcing she'd made Lerouge champion, had come two days ago. What a mercy that Hera Arvana had fulfilled the Founder's duty within the time allotted and before the draeden made any show of force.

Madra Cassandra lifted the small bell that rested on the wide arm of the Prioress's Seat, a heavy chair whose back was to the assembly so that she, as the other sisters, could face the Founder's icon during meditation. She rang the bell once, and it chimed so pure and clear in the confines of the room's stone walls. The sound would be lost in the wider world. So was the case with her soul. It had found within these walls its place to sound most pure and clear. She folded her hands and began to say aloud the closing prayer she had said thousands of times. Knowing it by rote, she ceased to hear her own chanting as she strove to feel the harmony made by the voices of the hundred women with her in the gathering room.

Illuminate our souls with Your Light,
You, in whom all is possible,
Dark and Light.
Judge and Forgiver,
Mother and Father,
Pour upon us that which in you is Love.
Use us for the purpose that your Wisdom chooses.
Draw us closer to you every moment of our life
Until in us is reflected your Joy and Peace
As it was in the Founder and the shacras.

In the silence after the prayer, the superior made her own petition for Prince Lerouge. She raised her gaze to the Founder's icon, and her heart went out to Hera Arvana. This duty had been a trial upon her protégé, but surely, by fulfilling her purpose, she was closer to joy and peace.

Over the muffled rustling of a hundred women trying to rise quietly, came the creak of the gathering room door, breaking the superior's concentration. An unsettling feeling overtook her as she gripped the arms of the chair, pushed up, and took the cane resting against the seat edge. Over the back of the Prioress's Seat, she saw a frazzled Hera Musette and the unsettled feeling turned to dread. What was so urgent to bring Hera Musette back so early in the day...and to violate the solemnity of the morning meditation?

"Please, you must come." Hera Musette's usually forceful voice came out in a plea so thin it nearly died in the air before it reached the superior.

In the hall, before the superior had time to ask why she had come at such an hour, Hera Musette blurted, "Forgive me, I know he shouldn't have been admitted beyond your offices, but I had him take Hera Arvana to her cell."

"Him?" the superior asked. "The prince?"

"Maker have mercy," Hera Musette said, then sighed. As they went through the halls, Musette alternately answered questions and told a story that brought the superior lower with each word until it ended with, "I pray we aren't too late for the last blessing. Surely she'll be far from the Maker without it."

The superior stopped, wobbled on her cane, and clutched Hera Musette's forearm. "Where is the relic?"

❖－❖－❖

Sharp cold panged through Arvana's shoulder. She fluttered her eyes open. It was Lina's ghost, pinching her shoulder. Arvana wondered how long she had been drifting in the strange sleeplike state. The last thing she remembered was Nan lifting her into Lady Martise's carriage. Nan. She wanted to see him, but everything beyond Lina, beyond Assaea's glow, was murky gray. She concentrated, tried to bring the world into focus. Still, everything was gray. Was she dead? Was this to be her doom for forsaking her vows? Being trapped in this place, unable to see anything except the sword of the man she loved. "Lina, am I dead?"

"No. I still see life in you, but some of your spirit is drifting away."

Drifting away? A knot of dread tightened in Arvana's stomach. When she died, her sins would pull her deeper into Hell, away from even this small connection to Nan. She wouldn't deserve that mercy. "I only—"

Lina held a hushing finger to her lips. "Someone is coming. Look."

A small blue light, the size of crown coin, shone above them. From it, a rush of life threads twisted and spun into the life-size form of a gaunt-cheeked old woman with sunken but bright eyes. The superior! She didn't wear her veil and the blue light emanated from her hand. It was the relic. For a moment, the superior was awestruck by Assaea's light, saying, "How amazing." But when she looked to Arvana, the lines about her mouth grew as grim and aged as a weathered fence post. With a kindly smile, she tried to cloak her initial expression.

"It's too late, isn't it?" Arvana asked.

"You've been here a long time."

"Cover it," Arvana said of the relic. She wanted to confess. Perhaps it would spare her from falling away from Nan completely.

Madra Cassandra nodded and shut the locket lid almost closed so The Scyon would not see them.

Arvana would've kissed the ground long and hard if she could. "I have failed in so many ways. I chose Prince Lerouge to take the Blue Eye, and now he's dead. And I broke my promise of constancy of heart. Take my ring. I don't want to die false to my vows."

"False?"

"I loved him. I put him before the Maker in my heart."

"And you do not repent this?"

"My repentance is never enough."

Arvana watched, but felt nothing, as the superior removed the ring from her finger. It was as if she was watching it happen to someone else.

The superior closed the ring in her hand. "What use is the Maker's forgiveness if you won't accept it?"

"Madra?"

"When your brother brought you here, he told me how your father died and how he blamed you. In his heart, he had to know he was wrong, but he was weak, couldn't bear to blame himself. It was easier to blame you, who would bear anything. And you, you look upon what you endured as a punishment, as if you deserved it. You won't accept mercy. Not for that. Not for forsaking your vows."

Though Arvana's living body seemed so distant, the past was as close as ever.

⚜ ⚜ ⚜

She was driving the sleigh. In the back sat her brother Allasan, his fiancé, Payter and Elizabetta. They were in the open country. The road ran in a long, straight stretch. With a flick of the reins, she urged the horses to go faster. She didn't know why she wanted to fly over the snow. It just was necessary to feel something, anything other than Payter's betrayal. How could he love Elizabetta? She cracked the reins. Snow stung her face and the wind whistled.

"What are you doing?" her brother shouted. "You'll put us in the ditch."

What *was* she doing? They could go in the ditch. With a tug on the reins, she slowed the horses to a trot. She'd never forgive herself if she hurt the horses...or anyone else. Even Payter or Elizabetta.

Their lane was ahead. She would go home and let Allasan drive. As she made the turn, something by the stable bounded from behind a snowdrift. She couldn't see it clearly through the snow. A dog? She halted the horses. They stamped and snorted restlessly. The animal loped into the lane. No, it wasn't a dog; it was a coyote. Why was it out in the middle of the day and why didn't it shy away as they always did?

It burst into a run toward them.

"Allasan," she screamed, but he was already beside her, grabbing the ax from under the front seat. He jumped from the sleigh. The spooked horses threw their heads up and began to retreat. The sleigh slid backward. They were angling toward the ditch. She sawed the reins, trying to steady them.

The coyote launched at Allasan.

One of the horses jerked in the harness. The rims of his eyes were white with terror. His front legs left the ground and circled in the air. The sleigh heaved to the side. They were going to overturn into the ditch.

She dropped the reins and leaped into the snow. She ran to the front of the team and grabbed their headstalls in either hand to hold them. "Easy, boys, easy." But the panicked horse threw his head back and his teeth flashed. He was going to rear. Her right arm snapped straight and her feet left the ground. The other horse's headstall ripped from her grip. She was dangling in air. Not weightless. All the weight in the world was pulling on her arm. She couldn't let go, couldn't fall beneath those frantic hooves, couldn't let the sleigh overturn.

"Whoa!"

Her feet sank back into the snow and she pulled the horse's head down by the headstall. "Good boy. That's my boy."

Allasan's hand joined hers on the wild horse's headstall. Steaming breath huffed from her brother's mouth. He gave a reassuring nod to his fiancée, then whispered, "That coyote was mad. I'm sure. Its eyes...its mouth...Ari...it had the mad disease."

"Allasan?"

"No, it didn't bite me. Now, let's get them away from *this*."

And then she saw it. *This* was bright red snow. *This* was the coyote, dead of a shattered skull. Her brother had been brave, then.

As they guided the skittish horses up the lane, she looked to the sleigh. Payter's cold-rosy cheeks had gone pale. Though the grain merchant's daughter was sobbing, he hadn't put his arm around her, wasn't holding her hand. He was a coward.

"Ari. Look." There was something brittle in Allasan's voice. It cracked as thin ice over a stream did underfoot.

Blotches of blood stained the trampled snow between the stable and the house. Blood streaked her father's guide rope. The coyote had been here first.

"Dear Maker, no," she said.

Allasan started running toward the house.

Then, everything disappeared into a blur of snow.

⚜-⚜-⚜

"If I had stayed home and done my chores, I would have seen the coyote," Arvana said to the superior.

"And perhaps died instead of your father? What would that have done to him, a man whose responsibility it is to protect his child? You dishonor him and the Maker."

Arvana knew, had always known, what the superior said was true, but it couldn't stop her from feeling that everything would have been different, good, if she hadn't chased after Payter, insisted on being a part of the sleigh ride her brother didn't want his younger sister tagging along on.

"The Maker sorrows over your father and your loss of him," the superior said. "Let that be your comfort, just as you let the Maker prop your strength when you stayed beside your father through the mad disease."

"Strength? I hated Allasan for leaving." Inwardly, she admitted why she loathed herself. It was something that couldn't be spoken: she'd wished over and over again that her father would just die when he thrashed with the mad disease, when he begged for water but couldn't bear to drink it. She had caused him this suffering and then couldn't even abide it. It was the worst selfishness.

"Would you have left your father if Allasan stayed?"

"It was my punishment." And she hadn't been able to willingly abide it. Just as she now didn't want to abide slipping farther away from Nan.

"But you stayed. Now, try to stay with us."

The superior went to reopen the relic when Lina flew to Arvana and said, "Promise me you'll take the relic." To the superior she added, "In my journals is the way to Alenius, the one with the Beckoner. I told my grandson to read them. They are in my trunk at Ferne Clyffe. What I revealed is worth more than a hundred thousand men."

The superior's widened eyes looked from Lina to Arvana. "You wish this task?"

"Madra, do you remember the translation of the book I sent you?"

"Of course."

"You can see the future. Look into the threads of my life and see if it possible. Ask with your heart."

"The glow of your life is weak, but I will try." Madra's brow knit while she peered into the possible paths of Arvana's life. Finally, she shook her head. "It is impossible to tell. There are too many possibilities. It isn't a simple yes-or-no question."

The glow of Assaea was still near. *He* was here. Up through the sorrow of her father's death welled a feeling of love. "I can't leave it to him alone. He has no chance against The Scyon without the Blue Eye."

Lina splayed her hands between them. "Take her back before it is too late. What is the sense in this?" Her ring, a cluster of sapphires and diamonds, seemed to flash with the woman's impatience.

The superior opened the relic's cover and curled a finger to Arvana. "Come home."

An excruciating pain, as if her whole body was being torturously squeezed, clenched Arvana. She screamed. The startling sound of it, coming from so far within her, dulled the pain for a moment.

From a distance came the sound of a door flying open. In a panic, Hera Musette shouted, "Madra Cassandra?"

"Out," the superior barked and snapped the locket closed.

Another wave compressed Arvana from head to foot. She scrunched her eyes shut and tensed. Waves of pain kept coming. Even Hell was better than this agony. "Stop, stop it." Her back arched from the bed. Her arms and legs burned. Involuntarily, she screamed again and wanted to thrash her limbs from her body.

"Soldier, help me," the superior said.

Arvana felt warmth around her shaking ankles, calming them. Gradually, the pain faded to an ache, and she relaxed into the lavender scent of the pillow. Was she home? She opened her eyes. It was dark but not gray. A slender column of light was breaking in though the gap between the drawn heavy drapes and fell across a familiar patterned stone floor. She was in her old cell. While bracing for another onslaught, she glanced to the superior, who was sitting in a chair beside the bed. She didn't glow with life as seen from Hell; she was pale and covered with a clammy sweat. Arvana marshaled her strength to raise her head. At the foot of the bed stood Nan, bent over and still holding her feet. Half of his hair had worked loose from its binding and obscured his face. "Madra, this is General Degarius."

As he righted, he flinched. He looked weary.

"Your shoulder," she said.

"I don't understand what happened," he replied.

"General, you are owed an explanation, but I ask you to wait. Your wound should be tended sooner rather than later," the superior said. "A monk from the other side of the valley has been summoned. He should be here now. After it is mended, you will take a room here to get rest. It would be cruel to send you to the other side of the valley now. Hera Musette," the superior called. The door opened and Musette hesitantly peered in. "Take the general to the infirmary."

"Nan," Arvana said. She wanted to thank him for bringing her here, but all he could do was give her a long backward glance as Musette led him away.

Her head dropped into her pillow. With Nan gone, the reality of where she was and what had happened closed in around her like the walls of the tiny cell that had once been her room. Chane was dead. Though Nan had killed him in self-defense, it was another death on his hands. It had all gone so wrong because she hadn't been staunchly true to her vows. "Madre, I have failed you...failed everyone. I—"

The superior raised her hand. "The world returned you to Solace wrapped in a soldier's black cloak. You have died to this life and the Maker has had mercy and granted you a new one. How are you to make it pleasing to the Maker?" She opened her palm. On it laid Arvana's silver novitiate ring. "From the first, I questioned your suitability to our life. Undoubtedly, you loved the Maker and wanted the Maker's love most fiercely. But, what happened to your father... Running away from things doesn't resolve them, but I thought I could help you, bring you peace. You were such an admirable novice that I almost forgot my reservation, even though you never confessed the things that lay heaviest on your soul.

"I meant to have a candid talk with you before awarding your veil, but then I saw you use the relic. You were the first, the only, in all my years as superior to see the blue glow when the stone was black." She opened the hand containing the Blue Eye and the other holding Arvana's ring. It seemed as if she were weighing the two. "I couldn't let you go. The Maker has corrected my mistake. In this new life, you are no longer a Solacian."

"Whatever you would have said to me, I wouldn't have left Solace as a novice."

Madra Cassandra kept speaking. "I never should have sent you to find a savior. As superior, the task was mine and now it returns to me. I must think on what you asked me in Hell. It is my decision. Does the general know what you carry?"

"No."

"You wrote me of his feat against the draeden and your certainty of his honor. He's the one who tested the constancy of your heart, isn't he?"

Arvana nodded.

"Is there any danger your feelings for the man influence your opinion of him? Hera Musette said he killed Prince Lerouge."

"It was self-defense."

One of the novices acting as porter brought in Arvana's bag and kithara from the cart and was about to set them down, but the superior shook her head. "Those things are of Solace. Take them to the storeroom."

"My kithara. It was my father's. It's my only remembrance." Her heart felt to break at the thought of losing it.

"How much are you willing to forsake to take the Blue Eye?"

She turned her face to the wall opposite the door. As painful as it was to lose the last link to her father, it was worse to think of Nan facing The Scyon alone. She wouldn't leave him as her brother had left her on the day their father went mad. "Everything. I will forsake everything."

"It may come to that," the superior said.

FIRST FLIGHT

The Forbidden Fortress, Gheria

We have been waiting for you. Just out of your bed? There are still pillow creases on your face." Sibelian smirked as he swung a burlap bag in his sole hand.

Rorke shuddered despite the warmth of his heavy velvet robe. Both Sibelian and the sovereign were standing at the edge of the draeden's pit. Had Sibelian played the waiting trick? And there was something gleefully ominous about that smirk and the way he swung the bag. Most troubling of all was the question of why they were gathered in the draeden's garden. Rorke glanced to the sovereign. There was no appearance of irritation in his eyes. To the contrary, they seemed to gleam with playfulness. "I came immediately." He felt his cheek and with an oblique nod to Sibelian said, "If there are creases upon my face, it is because I need more rest than those who stand around all day. My

Sovereign Alenius, I am always at your beckon at any moment's notice. How may I be of service?"

"Megreth will take to the sky today," the sovereign said. "We wished you to witness it."

Rorke relaxed. It was always dangerous playing with a madman. But, yet again he'd played his cards perfectly. It was the draeden's test flight, and Sibelian said no more. It was a good thing for the boy to hold his acid tongue. One too many provocations could prove to be his undoing once Rorke figured out how to use the Blue Eye. Despite a moon's time of trying, he'd not been able to unlock its secrets, though it did glow most amazingly in the dark. One day he'd figure it out completely, or the sovereign would explain it.

"Open the grate," the sovereign said.

Two soldiers on each side of the pit took up chains and began to drag the grate. The shrieking grind of metal on metal sent a delightful tingle down Rorke's spine. What a pleasure and honor it was to be among the very few to witness the draeden's first flight. Rorke clasped his hands beneath his stomach and felt the pleasantness of its weight and the thought that soon he would be the one ordering the grate open.

Pulled to the edge of the stone reflecting pool walls, the grate dropped with a thunderous *clang* to the ground.

The sovereign stepped to the edge of the pit. Though Rorke longed to join him, he stood his ground. It would look presumptuous to, without invitation, accompany the sovereign. The mask of humility was always a becoming one.

"Fare well, Megreth, my heart of flame." The sovereign raised his gloved hands and the head of the draeden, jet-black except for the ashy, white rims of it eyes, rose from the pit. Steam leaked from its nostrils. The sovereign turned his back on the creature and began to walk toward the stand of pines.

Seeing how Sibelian joined his father, Rorke abandoned his humility and trotted after them. Being left behind never brought one reward.

"Leave us," the sovereign commanded the soldiers who had manned the chains.

When he reached the trees, the sovereign turned around, closed his eyes, and clutched his chest as if he were in pain.

"My master," Rorke cried, but the sovereign took his hand from his chest and waved dismissively.

The sovereign opened his eyes and loosely rolled his shoulders, as if sloughing off the pain.

The draeden's head disappeared.

Was it frightened? How could such a magnificent beast be frightened? Well, perhaps of the sovereign.

In a burst, the beast exploded into the air. Its wings beat the air into a pulsing fury of dust and dead leaves.

Rorke laughed, then sucked in dusty air until he started to choke and cough. His eyes watered from tears of joy and from dirt. How the southerners would quake at seeing Megreth.

Finally, the air cleared. Far above, the draeden, its wings like black gauze lofting in the breeze, disappeared into the clouds.

Using his sleeve, Rorke wiped the grime and tears from his face. Who cared if it was his best robe? He'd have another made. And another. "How far will it go, my Sovereign?"

"To Acadia."

"Acadia?" Rorke asked. "I thought this was a test flight. The war isn't to begin until the Winter Solemnity."

"This is not war. It is a preemptive strike. He is going to Solace. He will have to stop and rest, but there are plenty of hants between here and there."

"A preemptive strike?"

Sibelian began to swing the burlap bag again.

In a pleased voice, as if he muttered to himself, the sovereign said, "I was right about him." In a less-pleased voice, he went on, "But it was the spy's fault. Aleniusson, return to our most loyal servant what is his."

Suspicion gripped Rorke, so deep his gaze froze on how Sibelian clasped the bag under his stump so he could angle the opening to the ground. It seemed to take an eternity.

To the ground fell the decayed head of the woman Rorke's spy had sent with the Blue Eye from Acadia. With a gut turning *thud*, Sibelian kicked it toward him. It came to rest at his feet. Rorke held his breath against the stench of decay.

The sovereign extended a gloved hand to him. "Let us see that locket you wear."

Before Rorke could unfasten the hook, the glove was at the side of his neck, grabbing the chain.

The chain dug into his neck, deeper and deeper into his flesh. He was about to buckle from the pain when the chain snapped. He touched his neck and felt the warmth of blood. *Why?* he wanted to ask. How had he displeased the sovereign? He'd been nothing but loyal.

Alenius opened the Blue Eye.

Was he going to take their souls? Rorke began to rear away and cower, raising his forearms to cover his face.

But the sovereign let go of the relic.

The Blue Eye landed in the baked-dry dirt.

Rorke peered from between his arms. The sovereign was grinding the relic with his heel. The sound of crushing glass and metal broke Rorke's hope into a thousand pieces. He dove to the ground and grubbed the dirt for the mangled pieces. "No! I am your most faithful servant."

"Don't worry, Rorke," the sovereign said all too happily. "It wasn't real. It was a good fake, though. The filigree and eye on the cover was correct. The inside even glowed in the dark. It fooled even us, for we cannot use it. A spyglass cannot be turned upon the spy's own eye. Whoever had it made had seen the real thing, had seen the real woman who carried it. The head you presented me from Acadia looked enough like the woman in our dreams. Your spy did half of his job. He found her."

"No."

"The real Blue Eye is in Solace. As the sun came up, as you were sleeping, we, too, were dreaming. In our dream we saw two women and a soldier. They could be anywhere, two women and a soldier. But then a third woman came into our dream. She wore the gray veil of the Maker's women. She said *Madra Cassandra*. So, you see, your spies failed you, tricked you. They sent you the head of another woman."

Alenius meant to destroy Solace and the Blue Eye, destroy Rorke's hopes. Rorke dropped to his knees beside the severed head. "Don't send the draeden to Solace. Let me go myself."

"Do you hold your wants over ours, faithful servant? We loathed to send our draeden to Shacra Paulus, for it would be a shame to destroy the monument that will bear our icons. But Solace? We shall burn it until they and their icons are nothing but ash. They would never have worshipped us, so let them be martyrs, burned past the point where even wax masks could be fitted to their faces."

Rorke wished he could eat his words, send them to his stomach to be digested and then shitted into a pot to be carried away by the lowliest of clerics. As he bent to the ground to kiss the dirt at Alenius's feet, his ear grazed the severed head. "Forgive me."

"You will kill your spy," the sovereign said, and then his boots left the small circle of Rorke's sight.

Rorke struggled onto his hands and knees.

Sibelian stood with a hardened smile. "You look like a dog. Take your bone." He kicked the severed head beneath Rorke.

"Help me up." To ask for Sibelian's assistance made Rorke's mouth taste like a mixture of dirt and rising bile.

"Maybe you should stay there, get more sleep." Sibelian walked away, Paulus's sword swaying at his side.

Rorke grasped the rotting head by its brown hair and flung it after Sibelian, but it landed far short and only earned him a mocking laugh. He got up on one knee, and grinding his teeth, pushed up from it with his hands. How had he been reduced to this indignity after the others he had suffered? The loss of his manhood. Dressing the corpse in the glass-topped casket. He'd lost the Blue Eye. No, he'd never had the Blue Eye. It was useless to mourn that, though he would kill Lord Sebastian for his treachery. No wonder the man had slipped off to Orlandia. He couldn't stay there, stay safe, forever. Nor could General Aleniusson stay safe. Rorke pooled the grit in his mouth and spit it after the general as if it were venom. The boy might have a priceless sword, but he didn't have the support of half of Gheria. He wasn't full-blood high Gherian. Many of the generals had secretly voiced their displeasure when Alenius had adopted him. What might not a few promises here and there do to persuade a regiment not to protect its commander? The boy already had lost an arm; he wasn't invincible.

Rorke dusted the dirt from his robe. He had, momentarily, like so many other times, lost his dignity—but never his cleverness.

DUSK

Solace, later that day

I t seemed to Degarius he'd slept only a moment when a voice was ordering him to wake. He cracked his eyes open. Light the color of dirty dishwater barely lit the room. Was it dawn or dusk?

"You must get up." He heard the woman's voice more clearly. Urgency filled it. It was Hera Musette.

Sitting up and reaching for his glasses sent a ripping pain across his back. Whatever the Solacian monk had given him to dull the pain of the stitches had worn off. An explicative was on his tongue, but he checked it. "What's going on?"

Hera Musette handed him a gray hooded tunic. He wasn't wearing a shirt.

"Where's my coat?" He looked to the side of the cot. No boots or sword. "What have you done with my sword?"

"It's safe and will be returned. Put on the tunic and come now," she barked like a sergeant, "if you want to keep your head."

"What?"

"Acadians."

Degarius, in the monk's tunic and sock feet, followed her through the maze of corridors. Behind them, an echoing clatter began. Boots rushing down a stairwell. Hera Musette clasped his hand and pulled him into a trot. They turned a corner. His sock feet slid over the worn-smooth stone, as if he'd hit a patch of ice. His hand tore free of hers and grasped at the air for balance. His knee crashed into the floor. Planting his palms on the floor, he sprang up.

Ahead, girls carrying baskets of apples were walking single file. Their eyes popped wide and they stopped. They thought he was chasing Hera Musette. Damn, if they screamed it was over. Hera Musette reached back to grab his hand again. She clasped her other hand over her mouth. Damn, the woman could think on her feet.

As they passed the girls, Hera Musette wheezed, "You saw nothing."

They raced down the corridor. How did a short, stout woman move so fast? Or had the draught made him slow? She darted into a narrow passage that led to a door. As she opened the door, a man's voice questioning the women resonated through the hallway.

Hera Musette closed the door behind them. It was a small chapel, filled with pillows for kneeling. Three ceiling-to-floor tapestries hung on one wall: Lukis, Paulus, and in the center, one of a grave-looking, gray-dressed woman. Hera Musette went to the one closest to the darkening windows, the tapestry of Paulus, and pushed it aside. Underneath was a half-sized door.

"Hurry, open it," she whispered.

Degarius pulled the handle. It was carved into the wood so the tapestry would lay flat against it. Hera Musette ducked inside, and he crouched to follow. Passing through, his shoulder scraped the doorframe. Grinding his teeth against the pain, he turned to ensure the tapestry was in place and closed the door.

They were at the top of a tight stairway ingeniously lit by windows high above. This time of day, it was nearly dark. He followed Hera Musette downstairs to a small, dirt-floored chamber in the footings of the building. In the dim light, he made out a long, low box shape in the center of the room. A crypt? Hera Musette knelt beside it and clenched her hands together. Degarius thought he heard a door open in the room above but couldn't be sure. Not trusting his hearing, he watched Hera Musette who was so focused she seemed to have stopped breathing. What was he to do if they found the door? They'd take him like a sheep for slaughter. They would take her for harboring a fugitive. Damn these Solacians. At least they could have left him his sword to go down fighting. He could pretend to have a knife and make a show of keeping her captive so they'd think her a hostage instead of an accessory.

Hera Musette's clasped hands drooped onto the crypt. "Blessed Founder, they're gone. Soldier, we must stay until the superior sends for us."

Degarius pressed his temples. "How could they know? No one saw it."

"What a gross violation to search Solace. Not that the superior would let them find anything. When the watch spotted the regiment coming up the road, she ordered your clothes burned in the kitchen fire and your sword put someplace safe."

Degarius's head swam. As he sat on the steps, his knee that hit the floor ached. So the redcoats hadn't found him today. They would sooner or later. He'd never make it to Sarapost with every redcoat looking for him—and every commoner, too. There would be a reward for his head. No, they wouldn't take his head. They'd parade him through Acadia, publicly humiliate him, and then torture him to death. He'd kill himself before giving that bastard King Lerouge the satisfaction of watching him die. But what if he did evade them and make it to Sarapost? Maybe—and it was a big maybe—for his father's sake, King Fassal would spare him if he understood he killed Lerouge in self-defense. With Acadia as Sarapost's key ally, however, even King Fassal wouldn't let him keep his generalship. That was gone. Even his captaincy was gone. The kitchen oven had burned his general's coat and his medals. They would be buried in the ash pile. What was left to him? Not staying here, even if it was the only safe place in the world. He hadn't prayed in over twenty years. There was no way in hell he'd start after this.

All of this was because of *her*. She'd had an affair with Lerouge. Hera Musette said so. It was why Lerouge put a knife in his back. Miss Gallivere might have insinuated about the wrong man, but she was right about the Solacian's character. And he had thought her good, had wrestled far into too many nights with the impropriety of his feelings. They were base desire, nothing more. The temptation of the forbidden. Damn her for what she'd put him through on the ride here. For everything she had cost him. Damn her to hell.

He slammed his fist backward into the stair's nosing.

JOINED AND ASUNDER

Lady Martise's, Shacra Paulus, the next day

For at least the tenth time, Fassal rose from his Aunt Martise's couch, shook his shoulders, and adjusted the cuffs of his sleeves so they just showed from his new deep plum-colored coat with cerulean buttons and fancy stitching. The Tierian waiting with him, a sullen lump of a monk with yellowed toenails, offered no diversion except his disgusting bare feet. Clearly, the monk had reservations—warranted ones for sure—about being here. Because of Prince Lerouge's death, Jesquin's father had refused to let the wedding proceed as scheduled, so his aunt had arranged this clandestine ceremony. Surely, she'd donated a vast sum to the Tierians, and taken on a great risk of the king's displeasure, to give them this one joy.

"Gregory," Aunt Martise had said yesterday, "with Sarapost heading into war, if something happens to you, I'd never be able to forgive myself if I didn't allow you this one joy."

Fassal needed one joy. Poor Degarius. All Fassal could do was shake his head in disbelief. What had happened still didn't seem possible.

Finally, the sitting room door opened, and Jesquin entered under the protective arm of his aunt. Suddenly, his nervousness was gone.

"Remember," Aunt Martise whispered to Jesquin, "not a word. Let me tell your father tomorrow."

Jesquin wriggled free of their aunt and came to Fassal. Plucking at the skirt of her black mourning dress, she turned her already moist eyes to him. "My wedding dress wasn't finished. It doesn't matter, does it?"

"You are beautiful, sweetheart," Fassal said into her ear and gazed into her eyes that for days had been awash in tears for her brother. Now they were wet with joy.

"And you're so handsome. Look at your coat." When she touched her forefinger to one of the buttons on his chest, he clasped her hand and kissed it.

The Tierian led them through the vows and pronounced them married.

"My dears, you have an hour," Lady Martise said. "Upstairs, the last room on your right is at your disposal."

Lady Martise held her smile while she listened to their rushed footsteps on the stair, and then she sank onto a couch. Dear Marslan could never return to Acadia, not after his son was accused of killing Chane. She could go to Sarapost, but what would become of Chane's little twins? They had no father now, and Jesquin must leave. King Lerouge had no time or patience for them. What was she to do? Go to Marslan or accept the only form of motherhood left to her?

Oh, how had all this happened? Yet again, Lady Martise wondered if she could have prevented it. Gregory told her that Marslan's son was in love with Hera Solace. She had thought to tell Gregory to warn the captain about Chane, but she decided it wasn't her place. Anyway, if Hera Solace had turned down Chane, why would she have the captain? The dinner with Teodor seemed to confirm Hera Solace's steadfastness to her vows. The captain had been out on the porch with her and came in looking dashed. But then, when the captain fell on the field to Chane, Hera Solace was much affected. There was something between them. Poor dears. What a struggle it must have been, and now this.

Lady Martise sighed. At least Gregory and Jesquin would be happy.

The superior's chamber, Solace

The knock on the door would be the monks come with Nan. Arvana refolded the letter from Lady Martise to the superior and extended it across the wide desk to her.

"Do you want me to tell him?" Madra Cassandra asked as she took the letter.

Arvana shook her head. Though she dreaded telling him, felt certain of his disappointment, she felt just as certain he would understand. It *had* been an accident.

"Then I'll give you a few minutes with him." The superior rose from the desk and shuffled toward her private rooms. "Enter," she called before leaving.

Four monks escorted Nan into the superior's chamber. He limped, worse than usual.

"Your feet?"

He said nothing, just stopped and glanced around the chamber, as if looking for someone or something, then not finding it, scowled, and rolled his gaze to the ceiling, the floor, to anyplace but her.

Arvana didn't think her heart could sink any lower than after she'd read the letter from Lady Martise, until she saw his utter coldness at seeing her. Did he already know, already blame her for everything he had lost?

"You may go," Arvana said to the brothers. "We shall be fine alone."

Nan stood straight and severe. "They said the superior wanted to see me."

"She does. She'll return shortly."

He pushed up his glasses. An ugly blue bruise covered the outside of his hand. Finally deigning to look at her, he caught her wondering stare. He turned his back to her and went to the window. Good. It would be easier not having to tell him to his face, not having those blue eyes that could be so inexplicably beautiful turn cold and pass judgment. "The superior just received word from Lady Martise. It explains the redcoats. They found your Valor in Service medal on the path. It's how they connected you with the prince's death. It's my fault. I must have dropped it. I'm sorry, Nan. I know the generalship means everything to you. There's a ten thousand crown reward—"

"My medal? So that's the explanation for *that*." He clasped his hands behind his back. "I suppose I can excuse that. You didn't intentionally leave it behind."

"Oh, Nan." Relief washed over Arvana. He did understand. She rose, began to go to him, but he slowly turned around and the look on his face was everything except forgiving.

"Now, tell me why Lerouge put his knife in my back in the first place."

"Nan?"

"A man died and I've lost *everything* for no reason other than jealousy. If I'd known you were his lover, I would've gladly made it clear he was free to have you. Gladly. Prince Lerouge. You might have mentioned it. The damned prince of Acadia..." He trailed off in disgust.

"Nan."

"What was I? Collateral in a game? One of us would give you a comfortable life. An enviable life. Not like this forsaken existence here."

"Let me explain! I never loved him."

"I don't doubt it." Gesturing to her ring-less hand, he said, "Now you are free to dupe some other man. What am I free to do? I regret pitying you. That's all it was, pity. I regret it in every possible way." The sharp, deliberate crispness in his voice was like the sound of a knife cutting an apple in halves that couldn't be rejoined.

Arvana backed to her chair.

The superior's chamber door creaked open and Nan looked away from Arvana, as if turning from a stranger. In the shock of his accusations, she hadn't had time to breathe, let alone think, and now the superior was here. Arvana wilted into her chair.

The superior motioned Nan to sit beside Arvana, but he remained standing. "I haven't detained you, spared you from the redcoats, on a whim," the superior said to him. "I know you killed a draeden and that your sword is Assaea."

Nan glared at Arvana, and she knew he was accusing her of yet another falsehood—sharing his secret.

"It was her duty to tell me," the superior said. "We know The Scyon and the draeden have returned. I sent her to the Citadel to find a savior to battle them."

"What?"

"She chose Lerouge. Now he's dead and time runs short. She told me you think war with the Gherians will begin this winter. It takes little to deduce they will use the fire draeden, which must be large and powerful by now. I am offering you the chance to take your sword against it and The Scyon."

"I never needed you to offer me the chance to take my sword against anything."

"Indeed." Just as she had the morning on the 5th of Spring when she laid the initial task on Arvana, the superior opened her desk drawer and withdrew a black box. "But you need me to offer you the Blue Eye, Lord Degarius." She lifted the lid. "The relic has been in our care since the days of the Founder. It is how we know The Scyon and the draeden are resurrected. Anyone who can use the relic can see them through it. With my own eyes, I saw a poor, pitiful girl birth the two demons. One was put in a silver bowl of water; the other they laid upon a brazier."

"A girl?" Degarius asked. The appalling thought of a girl having to bear monsters softened his stiff defensiveness.

Arvana shuddered and touched her hand to her stomach. A girl had to lay with The Scyon, carry the evil within her, and then birth them. Perhaps as an act of mercy, the superior had never told her that. But she told Nan.

The superior continued, "With my own eyes, I have seen The Scyon, though he hides behind a black hood."

"Black hood," Nan said. "Alenius, the Gherian Sovereign, has taken to wearing a hood, but I guess it would be blue, and is claiming that he's divine."

"Color is difficult to discern in the dark. It must be him. Then you know where to find him?"

"The Forbidden Fortress," Nan muttered, and he came to the desk and peered inside the box. " So that's the Blue Eye." His eyes narrowed and shifted to Arvana. "Lerouge had that when he died. You gave it to him because he beat me in the tournament."

"No, Prince Lerouge made that test for himself," Arvana said. "I gave it to him because you couldn't use it. I hoped you could, prayed you could, because I knew you could be trusted with it. But I tested you with it at Bonfire Night and you saw nothing. I even looked to see if I could make you use it—as the Judges made other Judges—but the trial would break you, ruin your body and mind. With all my heart, I wanted to give it to you."

"Lerouge hasn't seen a fraction in his life of what I have."

"I know. I have wondered the same myself. But perhaps it is what you see in death."

"Then why the hell am I here?"

The superior pushed the relic box toward Arvana. "Because Miss Nazar can use it."

Arvana felt a stab at being called Miss Nazar. She didn't know who Miss Nazar was. She had always been plain Ari or Hera Arvana. It hadn't quite seemed like she renounced her vows until this moment. Though she had relinquished her ring and left behind her silver headband and veil at Lady Martise's, she still wore her gray habit; she had nothing else. Even the kithara was no longer hers.

"*Her?*" Nan growled the word.

"Through the Blue Eye I saw you kill the poison draeden. I saw its spirit enter Hell. It is why I hoped so much that you could use the relic."

"I killed it for certain?"

"For certain. I knew from the start, from when Prince Fassal mentioned why you earned the Valor in Service medal. When I saw your sword, it confirmed it."

Nan sank into the chair. "But I can't use the Blue Eye."

"Prince Lerouge took her into Hell with the Blue Eye," the superior said. "It was why you had to bring her to me...to retrieve her. She survived there longer than I would have thought possible. Her body, like none other, is hardened to the shock of having had its soul in Hell."

"Lerouge nearly killed her with that thing," he said.

"Prince Lerouge defeated you once, too," Arvana said quietly.

"You propose I stroll into Gheria with *her*?" He addressed the superior only.

"Your grandmother promised a great help. She said you would know what it is...something you read in her journals."

"My grandmother?"

"She is in Hell. She lingers in the light of your sword. It is truly blessed."

"Surely there is someone else to take the Blue Eye and better counsel than that of a dead, mad woman." Crossing his arms, he asked, "And if I refuse this lunacy?"

"Your sword still goes north, albeit in less skillful hands," the superior replied. "You know too much. You must stay with the brothers until either the war ends or a draeden comes. Those of faith are always among their first targets."

"You give me no choice."

Arvana opened her hands in her lap. "I wish there was time to find another champion. I never wanted to take the Blue Eye, but have accepted it." It didn't seem the right time to tell him that she'd pledged to Lina that she'd help him. The last thing he'd appreciate now was any obligation she felt toward him. "What else is there to do? The fire draeden will be upon us. What if The Scyon breeds more draeden? A wasting draeden? And time runs short. Can you tell me who could be trusted with it? In the wrong hands—"

One of his nearly invisible brows arched as he turned to her. "Yours are the right ones?"

"No mortal since the Judges has used the Blue Eye more than I have." Arvana garnered her conviction. "You hesitate because I am the last person with whom you would wish to undertake anything. I swear I will never mention our past. This is about far more than us."

He scoffed. "I refuse because it's a ludicrous idea. If I were a general, had an army like Lukis and Paulus, perhaps I could breach the walls of the Forbidden Fortress. Oh, then there is the fact that I have a price on my head. To avoid the main roads, we'll have to take the Verdea Crossing, go through Cumberland to Sarapost. It is full of unmarked hants and bandits. And entering the Gherian

Forbidden Fortress with only one sword and a woman—"

The sound of the superior edging her chair from the table interrupted him. "I understand you've decided, Lord Degarius. I'll call the brothers to escort you to your cell."

Nan jumped to his feet. "No monk touches my sword. I said you gave me no choice. Give me a good bowman. My shoulder is too stiff to draw."

The superior rose, bowed to Nan, took the locket, and shuffled around the desk. "Rise, Arvana Nazar. As the Founder entrusted the relic to Paulus, I entrust it to you. Maker have mercy on the sins you must bear for our sake."

The superior hung the locket once again around Arvana's neck. The first time she'd done so last spring, her skin had shivered at its coldness between her breasts, and at the strange mix of trepidation, obligation, and hope with which she accepted the duty she'd secretly hoped would make her a shacra. Then, over the summer, it had grown as familiar as her novice's ring, sitting against her skin without notice. Now, in taking it, she felt nothing except numbing resignation. What had she expected? For happiness to come from the breaking of her vows? For this terrible task to be a honeymoon?

"I wish you to leave as soon as possible," the superior said. To Nan she added, "Make a list of what you need. Solace will provide coin and whatever is necessary."

Nan raked his fingers through his hair. "I have to go home to Ferne Clyffe. I've never read my grandmother's journals."

BURNING

Outside of Solace, the next morning

Though Degarius's knee was swollen and stiff and his shoulder wound throbbed, he was glad to be out of Solace. He rubbed his forehead under his Solacian monk's gray wool cap. It itched, but did a good job of hiding his telltale hair. The morning sun was flickering through the half-bare autumnal trees that lined the secluded, rambling path along the hillsides outside of Solace. Eventually they would have to join with the road that led to Verdea Crossing, but by then, his beard would be full and a bright red. No one in Acadia, except Fassal, knew it was that color. For now, they were safe, but slow.

For disguise and the convenience of riding, Miss Nazar was dressed as a monk, too. Miss Nazar. It sounded strange, but what the hell else was he supposed to call her? She wasn't Hera Solace anymore. How had he even started calling her *Ari*?

He never called Miss Gallivere *Esmay*. Miss Nazar sped her horse to a trot to jump a fallen tree in the path. She leaned forward and was up and over the log. He had never campaigned with a woman in tow. It was sure to be a pain, but at least she was an accomplished rider. He couldn't fault that skill or complain that she couldn't keep up because she was ill. Despite the dark circles under her eyes and a hollowness to her face, she rode diligently.

Degarius took his turn jumping the tree. Even though his knee ached when he rose in the saddle, the motion felt good, full of freedom after the confinement to the monk's cell. But as he looked back to ensure that Heran Kieran, the Solacian brother following with the pack animal, made it around the log, the sense of freedom left as quickly as the exhilaration of jumping the horse. He wasn't free. He had to abide the superior's plan...for now. If he reached Sarapost, he could take the relic to King Fassal. The Sarapostans would find someone better than Miss Nazar to use it, and he might earn his generalship back as recompense. As Miss Nazar said, this was about more than them.

The path widened and Heran Kieran, who was assigned as their archer, came alongside. He was a young man, well made and with dark skin suited for even the strong Orlandian sun. The superior had allowed Degarius to watch a demonstration of the man's skill before accepting him into the party. The man's speed and accuracy were better than even Salim's. "Your archery skill would've earned you a commission in the Acadian army."

Kieran tilted his head thoughtfully, as if the idea had never occurred to him. "That would have displeased the Maker. It's wrong to kill even an animal in sport."

Degarius bristled. What misguided mentality thought soldiering a sport? No frontiersman under his command would've dared speak to him with the heran's zeal and conceit. But, he wasn't the captain, not in title. Someone must be in charge of this regiment. Though Miss Nazar held the Blue Eye, he had all the expertise. As he did in assessing his new men at the start of a patrol, he stowed Kieran's remark and Miss Nazar's riding abilities into his mind like blankets into a pack. He didn't have to like the man; his being a good archer and a presence besides Miss Nazar were enough.

An orange flash flitted in the corner of his eye. Degarius glanced to the sky. It was an even, cloudy gray. The sun couldn't have broken through. Miss Nazar had stopped, was watching the sky, too. He hadn't imagined it.

The glow again lit the clouds. It moved, disappeared, and then glowed again. What the hell?

Out of the clouds dipped a black form, like a bat, but a thousand times larger. His horse jerked its head.

It had to be a draeden, but a dozen times more immense than the one in Lake Sandela Hant. Degarius's feet throbbed.

The draeden burst into a blinding light as if it was lit kindling. Heat waves swam in the sky. The treetops under the creature burst into flame. A hot breeze, like a blast of air from a furnace, rolled over. "Take cover," he shouted and steered his horse deep into a stand of pines. Miss Nazar joined him, the Blue Eye in hand, her thumb on the latch. Heran Kieran, with the packhorse, slipped in with them.

Degarius grasped Assaea's hilt, but the sudden backward thrust of his arm sent pain shooting through his shoulder. He stopped. What good would the sword do, even if he were full strength? For all love, the draeden mustn't see them or be enticed to them with the relic. "Don't try to use it," he said to her.

Heran Kieran, who'd drawn a bow and held it aimed to the sky, looked desperately to them. Didn't the man understand the damn thing would incinerate them before they could get close enough to engage it? It would be pure foolishness to tempt it to them. On the hillside, there'd be nowhere to hide from the heat. It would have every advantage.

A curtain of smoke rose in the distance.

"Solace. It must have attacked Solace," Heran Kieran cried. "We must ride back to see if we can help."

Degarius, perched on his horse, listened with the air of a lieutenant awaiting an order—however foolish it might be. Miss Nazar's sentimentality would send them on a pointless errand. Solace's forested ground was kindling. He would negate the order, of course, but he wanted to hear it first. Then, there'd be no doubt of who led this little regiment.

Miss Nazar couldn't tear her gaze from the smoke, not until Heran Kieran rode from the pines, his horse poised to retrace the path to Solace.

"Heran, there's nothing we can do," she said.

"But they'll—"

"It was looking for us," she said. "Stay in the trees until we're sure it's left."

As Kieran returned to them, his eyes hardened on Miss Nazar. "Couldn't you have stopped it? Isn't that why you have the Blue Eye?"

Before she could answer, Degarius said, not to defend her, but to defend his decision not to engage it, "With our weak vantage point, we would have been incinerated." At the word *incinerated*, his feet burned as they had the night he narrowly escaped Lake Sandela.

❦ ❦ ❦

Degarius had amassed a lead on the Gherian horsemen and veered onto a path into a wood. He wanted to stop and pull off the boots. His heels burned as if he was holding them to a flame. But it wasn't safe yet. They traversed two brooks before reaching a middling-sized stream the horses easily forded. Coming out upon the other side, they kept to the path until it reached a relatively dry plateau where the horses' hoofprints wouldn't be so marked. He stopped, and turning around, said to Salim, "We're going back to the stream and following it through the woods." His hope was that it would take the Gherians a while to figure out that they'd backtracked and followed one of the streams instead of the path.

The horses trudged along the sandy-bottomed shallow stream until it flowed into a larger one. Here, finally, was one bit of luck among so much very bad luck. "This stream takes us in the general direction of the Outpost," Degarius said. "If the Gherians follow, at least it won't be the whole lot of them. They'll have split up to cover the area. Do you hear anything?"

Salim turned his head from side to side like a wild beast as he struggled to hear beyond the dripping trees. "Not for now."

"I think it's safe to water the horses," Degarius said. He dismounted. When his boots hit the ground, excruciating pain shot up through the soles of his feet. His knees began to give. Clenching his teeth, he threw his arms over True Pearl's back to alleviate the pressure and gain a moment to recover. "Steady, girl."

Salim was at his side, locking his arm around his.

"Damn it, get off me," Degarius growled, but Salim was lowering him to the ground. Sitting, he cringed and leaned to take off a boot. One tug and his mind went white with pain or was it the light Salim was making. Damn him, making a light.

His head swimming, Degarius leaned back onto his elbows, and then sprawled on his back. He could hear Salim whispering, but his voice seemed unreal, distant, like something he was remembering.

"Let's see what's wrong," Salim was whispering. "Oh, Maker."

❦ ❦ ❦

Oh, Maker, indeed. It had cost Degarius two excruciating months for his feet to heal and to force himself to walk upon the tight, fragile, sensitive new skin. What massive damage this fire draeden could do not to just one man, but to an entire army.

As if he hadn't spoken of their poor vantage point as the reason for not engaging the beast, Miss Nazar said to Kieran, "It was too far away. There was nothing I could do."

"How close to you have to be?"

"Close."

Maybe there was wisdom in trying to sneak into Gheria, Degarius thought.

Out of the smoke over Solace, the draeden reappeared. With a few hard flaps of its wings, it gained altitude and disappeared into the clouds, which didn't periodically glow anymore. "It is returning to Gheria," Degarius said. "Hopefully it thinks whoever planned to use the Blue Eye is dead. We'll have the advantage of surprise, which we'll need to get close." Close enough for a sword. Close enough for a Blue Eye.

"As long as I don't have to use it," Miss Nazar said, "we will have the advantage of surprise."

Degarius nodded. The draeden gone, his concern turned to the trees smoldering in the valley below. "Let's go. I don't want to get caught in a fire."

For dinner, Kieran passed out the cloth-wrapped pastries from Solace and bottles of ginger beer, then closed his eyes to make a prayer of thanks. Out of habit, Arvana closed her eyes too, but no prayer came. She felt empty, as if someone had gouged her and the one small draught of spirit she had left had leaked out. If her soul had been overflowing, she'd have borne it, found consolation in the reserve. Her sinful love of Nan, the suffering over leaving the order, and Chane's death, had each consumed a portion of her soul. She was unworthy of mercy so it never replenished. What was left drained away with the burning of Solace. Only now did she truly see how wrong it had been of her to love Nan. His bravery and handsomeness weren't permission for her to break her promise to the Maker. Even as he had renounced his love for her at Solace, she had kept a kernel of hope that there was something worthy, enduring in what had been between them. But now she saw it for what it was—wrong. She had no right to call him by his child name. He must be Degarius, or Lord Degarius. He had always been the one to do the moral thing. He was the one who was adamant about the choices in life he'd made for his career, the one who stopped coming to the archive, the one who had tried to keep their last meeting unemotional. And because she'd been too weak to abide, Chane was dead, Nan—*no, Degarius*—had lost his generalship, and the worst of all, Solace was burned. The Scyon had learned who they were when the Hera Musette, unknowingly, called to the superior while the Blue Eye was open. Did the superior know the draeden was coming? Had she evacuated the valley? *No, she sacrificed them so that The Scyon would think whoever had the Blue Eye was dead.* The Solacians didn't deserve that fate, to suffer for another's sins. Where was the Maker's mercy? Was there even a Maker? Perhaps all that was beyond was Hell. Perhaps the swords weren't blessed, but merely clever manmade instruments like the Beckoner and Blue Eye.

A cork popped from a bottle of ginger beer. Arvana opened her eyes and so did Kieran. "Don't let me interrupt you," Degarius said and took a long drink.

"You may join us in prayer," Kieran replied with the irritating self-assurance of a man who had no doubt of how he stood with the Maker.

Degarius shook his head to Kieran's invitation to pray. "Pray to a Maker who lets things happen like what happened today?"

"Men caused what happened today."

Drumming his fingers on the bottle, Degarius said, "Then I don't see the point of praying."

"We pray for perseverance to do the right thing when our freewill allows the wrong. Even over something as simple as a meal, we can choose to eat it without consciousness of the labor and life that went into it, or we can be mindful of it."

"A man doesn't need to pray to know those things."

"Different men need different things. I congratulate you if your soul is a model of perfection."

Degarius looked over his glasses and chewed his lip. Whatever he was going to say, she didn't want to hear it or any more of this conversation.

"I never—" Degarius began.

She stood and held her still-wrapped food to Kieran. "Save it," she said as much of the food as their argument. None of it mattered.

"You must eat to be strong enough to ride," Kieran said in refusal. "You've been ill."

"I've never been too ill to ride," she grumbled.

Both men looked at each other and Degarius raised a brow as if he begged to differ. Yes, he'd had to carry her to Solace. But, there was a vast difference between being ill and being dead. She tossed the wrapped food to Kieran.

EFFIGY

Forbidden Fortress, that evening

The eunuchs and Fortress Guards are so full of wine they're pissing on her," Alenius said with glee to Sibelian at the sight of his clerics raising their robes and aiming their steams at the effigy, a woman's form sewn of sack-cloth, stuffed with straw, and dressed in a plain gray dress that was now darkened with streaks. It was one thing men and half men could do together. Having drunk a bottle Gherian burned wine before summoning his court to the plaza in front of the Worship Hall, Alenius's own bladder was full and ached to empty on the hanging image of his enemy. It would be a fitting gesture before the grand end to the celebration. He strode to the effigy, taking pleasure in the sensation of his robes billowing behind from the breeze and the masterfulness of his stride. He felt like his draeden must when skimming the sky.

With a cheer, the crowd of clerics and guards made way for him. When Alenius reached the effigy, Rorke appeared from the crowd. "Turn your backs, servants of the divine. Bow your heads and close your eyes. You are not worthy to witness the glory of the sovereign."

Despite his disappointment, what a dedicated servant Rorke is, Breena whispered into Alenius's thoughts.

Not wanting to think of Rorke, Nils, or any concern other than pissing, Alenius blotted the words from his mind and pulled up his robe. He took his manhood in hand and sent a strong stream up the front of the effigy. He laughed as it reached the crudely painted face. A mixture of relief at the emptiness and pride at the youthful power of his flow made him feel more alive than ever. And now that the Blue Eye and those who kept it were destroyed, no one could take that sensation from him ever again. Not the wickedness of his mother against Breena. Not age. He shook off the last drops and released his robe. "Who shall execute the whore who drank of the divine?"

The clerics and Fortress Guards opened their eyes, turned around, and with bellicose shouts each clamored for the executioner's duty.

Except for Nils. Away from the crush of clerics, he sat hunched over his cane, with a young eunuch, upon the low stone wall around the plaza. Alenius's soaring spirit dipped. He wished he hadn't seen Nils; he'd just vowed not to think of him. Yet, his conscience had taken his gaze directly to his old friend. Despite all his power, Alenius couldn't stop the effect of time on mortals. Such was the burden on the divine, to be untouched by time but to bear witness to it. *I shall let Nils execute the woman.*

Nils? Breena asked. *He won't even notice what is happening. He has the young cleric trapped in conversation.*

That was true. Once he had someone's ear, Nils always rambled about the old times. It was as if he were locked in a prison of his own past and had seen nothing of the current world for years. Not that long ago, Alenius reflected, he too had been fond of such talk. Now, he knew the young cleric wished nothing more than to escape and join his peers. It would be foolish to waste today's honor upon Nils. *Who should I choose?*

Why choose? Give Sibelian and Rorke each a part, Breena said.

Both? Breena had finally come to appreciate his adopted son. Sibelian had found Assaea whereas Rorke had been tricked by the spy. But Rorke had lost much and this was a small compensation for his continued loyalty. "General Aleniusson and Our Excellency Rorke, we command you to execute this woman."

At the mention of Aleniusson's name, a wild hurrah came from the Fortress Guards. The clerics clapped in unison for Rorke.

Nils lifted his bald head. Did he understand what was happening? The downward drag of guilt further grounded Alenius's high spirits.

And what of Sibelian? He was standing as solemn as one of the statues of the ancestors peering down from over the massive arched doors to the hall. At Alenius fixing his gaze on him, he finally started toward the effigy.

My love, he doesn't seem happy about the honor you give him.

Indeed, Sibelian looked putout and a faint hint of disgust played on his lips, as if this celebration was beneath him.

Perhaps he doesn't stand and make water like a man, Breena said. *Or perhaps he knows that with the Blue Eye destroyed you are invincible, and he is forever doomed to only be a viceroy.*

It was an unthinkable accusation, that his own son would have used the Blue Eye against him. *He has proven his loyalty*, Alenius thought staunchly, though anger at his son simmered in the pit of his stomach. Why must the boy always appear such an ingrate? It was the way of youth, but after two treks to the frontier, Sibelian's soft youthful features had firmed. He should have known how to act the part of a man of honor.

Sibelian has proven his loyalty for the rewards of a generalship and a priceless sword. Ask of him a sacrifice that you yourself made and see if he can abide it. Ask him to live a life without love. Rorke has already made that sacrifice.

I won't castrate my son.

No. Breena laughed her sweetest laugh. *I would never ask you to do that. Sibelian has lost enough of his body. I mean his soul.*

※ ※ ※

"What did the sovereign say?" Nils asked the cleric at his side, a recently made eunuch who had been an asher under Rorke. "Why the cheering?"

"They are going to burn the effigy."

"Help me up. I need to go to the front."

The boy bent and offered his elbow.

Nils grumbled that he should have gone forward earlier. Alenius would have offered him the honor of setting the effigy aflame, for he still was the ranking cleric though the sovereign had taken Rorke into his confidence. And, after all, he was the one who had supervised the Lily Girls' sewing of the effigy. Wasn't he? Or had he just heard them speaking of finding the sackcloth? In any case, once the pissing started, he'd retreated to sit on the wall, embarrassed that he'd have had nothing to add except a stinking puddle on the plaza stones. Watching his step by prodding the uneven pavers with his cane, he edged toward the clerics and

Fortress Guards who circled the effigy. Upon
reaching them, they stepped aside. Nils looked up.
Aleniusson, Rorke, and the sovereign were
gathered at the feet of the effigy, which was
propped upon a post.

"General Aleniusson, are you my son in every
way?" the sovereign asked.

Sibelian put his single hand to his chest and
bowed.

"Then swear to me that this woman is your love
and that you'll never marry another."

"What woman?" Sibelian asked and began to
look about.

Though Nils knew who the sovereign meant and
why, he said nothing; Alenius never liked his
surprises to be spoiled. Nils smiled to himself. He
had never particularly liked Sibelian; the boy never
seemed to appreciate the riches heaped upon him
simply because he bore a resemblance to the
sovereign. Now that resemblance was going to cost
him dearly.

The sovereign pointed his gloved finger at the
effigy.

"She's the enemy," Sibelian said.

"Surely your charm would have won her to our
cause."

"She's dead."

A hushed snicker went around until the
sovereign, with all seriousness said, "Love never

dies. If you are my son, fall to your knees and pledge your love."

Sibelian slowly sank to his knees.

"Rorke, lead him through his marriage vows."

Rorke? Why Rorke? Nils knew the words to the vows. He began them in his mind, reciting the first passage, but when he came to the second, the words disappeared as if they'd been rubbed out from a wax tablet and only vague gouges were left were the letters had been. As he tried to decipher them, he heard Rorke already speaking, pronouncing the words with relish, and Sibelian mumbling the promises to provide home and hearth.

Sibelian finally rose.

"You know that she will die a fiery death," the sovereign said. "Spare her from it. Use your sword."

The plaza was so quiet that Nils swore he could hear the *swoosh* of the sword leaving the sheath and the *crunch* of it piecing into the bodice of the hay-stuff effigy. A wad of gagging phlegm rose in Nil's throat. He'd seen many executions, but the first had been Breena's—a mercy killing. As Alenius's best friend, he stayed at his side when he stabbed Breena to put her out of suffering from the burns. To this day, the thought of it made his stomach sour. He coughed and spit.

"Ah, Nils. Bring us the torch," said Alenius. "The woman must burn. It is her fate."

In the thrill of hearing the sovereign acknowledge him, Nils forgot the twisted emotions of a moment ago. He drew himself up as tall as his bent back would allow. He was still above Rorke; the sovereign needed him. A Fortress Guard presented Nils with a long torch. Not trying to lean too heavily upon his cane, he shuffled to the effigy and was about to touch the torch to the hem of the woman's dress when the sovereign said, "Give it to Rorke."

❦ ❦ ❦

As the fire spread from the dress to the stuffed sackcloth body, Alenius felt all the dread he feared. The burned wine and pissing had momentarily taken his mind from the memories he knew the burning of the effigy would ignite. As it burst into flame, making an orange glow against the sunset, he remembered Breena's suffering. He had steeled himself somewhat against it. He knew Breena insisted on burning the effigy because she understood the pain the flames represented and wanted to see it visited upon their enemy. What he hadn't been able to anticipate was her test of Sibelian's loyalty, how it brought back the guilt he felt in killing her with his own knife. He had done it just as much to end his own suffering as hers.

My love, Breena said, *I have always only thanked you for taking my life. It was hopeless. Perhaps it was wrong of me to remind you of that time, but I had to know Sibelian was with us. It was for his own good. With no heirs, the common people of Gheria will never begrudge him his position. We must do everything to ensure that he is respected as viceroy.*

He will be respected when we show ourselves divine.

Still, many of the cabinetmen will plot against him. He's not full-blood. There's only one solution.

What is that? Alenius asked.

Kill the cabinetmen and their tradition of privilege. Poison their wine at our feast during the Winter Solemnity.

Only a few cabinetmen object to him. Why poison so many who support him?

What do you value more? The approval of seventy-five cabinet men or the love of a million commoners. They despise the cabinetmen.

Alenius hesitated. The cabinetmen contributed huge sums that supported the army and the Forbidden Fortress.

My love, with the world at your disposal, why do you need the gold of men who fancy themselves your advisors? You need neither their coin nor opinions. You will be benevolent to all.

Yes, Breena, I will be.

To all except your enemies.

MOON BLOOD

Two weeks later, near Verdea Crossing

"U rsatka mig." Miss Nazar said excuse me
in Gherian and gingerly dismounted
for the third time that morning. Her
accent was decent, and she had readily
learned the words Degarius offered.

Heran Kieran halted to take her horse's reins.
"*Some do omskart.*"

Degarius cringed. The monk might be a man of
peace, but he butchered the Gherian language by
insisting on using the same cadences as Anglish.
Degarius had tried to make him hear the
differences dozens of times. It was useless. If they
went into Gheria, Kieran was going to have to
pretend to be mute.

It was Miss Nazar's idea for them to learn
Gherian. Until he was certain he could overpower
Kieran, he had to pretend he was going along with
the plan of them going into Gheria as a paltry

threesome force. As taxing as it was to work with Kieran, an unexpected benefit was that it somehow made speaking with Miss Nazar easier. Not that she spoke to him often or unnecessarily. She was too proud. There'd be no pleasantries aimed at warming his affections; she was the kind of woman who wouldn't bear being dismissed twice.

But now, she'd asked to be excused, again. Unattended illnesses, like diarrhea, could grow worse and stop their progress. So much for insisting that she was never too ill to ride. Well, she was still riding, but it was taking forever with these frequent stops. "Perhaps you should take something," he called after her in Anglish so she would be certain to understand.

She stopped and turned. "Take something?"

"What did your apothecary send," he asked Kieran. "Miss Nazar is ill."

She lowered and shook her head. "It's not illness. Because I wear breeches, perhaps you forget I'm not a man. How am I to say it?" She spiked the toe of her boot in the dirt, blurted, "It's my time," and darted into the woods.

Degarius pulled his hat to the top rim of his glasses. What kind of blockhead did she take him for? Breeches did nothing to disguise she was a woman; they made it more obvious, gave exact shape to what he'd only imagined. When she was out of sight, he groaned.

Kieran said, "It's normal for a woman who's not with child."

Degarius groaned again. "I'm aware, Heran." It was beyond imagining that a chaste brother ventured to teach *him* of women.

Upon returning and remounting, Miss Nazar asked, "What's the Gherian term for a woman's time?

"*Dien efin.* Moon blood." Degarius's face went hot.

"Your knowledge of Gherian is comprehensive," Kieran said.

For once, Kieran said something Degarius was glad to hear—a change in subject. "I learned Gherian at the age where children are curious about life."

"I've always thought it's a pity that learning the meaning of words usually does little to give them value, or to guide one morally through life."

Another barb at him? The brother was looking at Miss Nazar, not him. Funny, he'd assumed there would be sympathy between them because of their backgrounds. Was this about how easily she'd learned Gherian? Or because she'd spent her time in Solace learning Old Anglish—then resigned. Of course, Kieran didn't approve. He probably blamed her for what happened at Solace, too.

"One uses words, Heran," she said, "both internally and externally to frame moral questions.

How can one do so without awareness of their meaning?"

"In the moment of truth, we find words teach one nothing," Kieran said. "Who hasn't acted solely on wordless, primal feelings and urges? In such cases, the state of one's moral center determines if the resulting action is good."

What in all hell was that about? Had the blasted superior inflicted this man on them as a punishment for that one moment Lerouge found them in? Had Miss Nazar told the superior about that, too? At least in his case, it had come from an honest feeling, even if it was only pity. Well, the monk and Miss Nazar could argue all they wanted about theology when he left them at Ferne Clyffe.

❀ ❀ ❀

Verdea Crossing

Town—beds, baths, and a few hours break from the saddle. Even as a girl Arvana had never ridden so much.

Just ahead, Verdea Crossing lay like a patchwork blanket before the Black Top Mountains. They'd surely overnight in an inn. The superior had returned a portion of Arvana's novitiate's fee and added a fair sum for the others. Her purse held plenty of crowns to pay for beds and hot baths. What a treat it would be to peel off the road-weary tunic, soak off the week's worth of dirt and moon blood, then slip into a bed. But as they neared the town gate, Degarius tucked all his hair under his hat and stashed his glasses in a pocket. Her small pleasure of anticipating a good night's sleep dissipated. This was no treat for him. He worried he'd be recognized. They'd avoided any settlements so far, but they needed supplies and the tunnel at Verdea Cross was the fastest, easiest way into Cumberland.

He rubbed his bearded chin. The beard *did* go a long way as a disguise. The redcoats would be looking for a blond man. The beard was reddish and made him look older, worn. Or perhaps the grimace from squinting was what aged him.

The people gathered at the gate, including three redcoats, looked at them as people always look at monks—wanting to stare but embarrassed to be noticed doing so.

Inside the gate, houses of rough-hewn timber lined the street. Keithan had been from Verdea Crossing. He might have grown up in one of these very homes. His parents could be living here still. What remembrance of him would console his parents? She couldn't tell them how he'd rescued her from the stream at Summercrest and taken Chane away. Perhaps the best she might offer was that he was like a brother to her. The idea of finding his parents, however, had to remain only an idea.

A warm, yeasty smell interrupted the thought. Her mouth watered.

Degarius's eyes squinted even harder. "Do you see a bakery?" he asked Kieran.

"Ahead, on the left."

They tied the horses to a post. Degarius divvied the supplies each should procure. To her disappointment, except for the apples and bread she was to get, it was more of the dried foodstuff they'd already been eating.

With two long loaves in her backpack, she left the bakery and bit into a bun she'd bought for herself. Nothing tasted as good as plain bread with a hard crust and airy center. As she let a bit of crust soften in the roof of her mouth, she looked into the next-door shop's window. A delicate blue caught her eye. Among the fancy chemises and pelisses hanging on display was a robin-egg-blue nightgown. After wearing for three weeks men's leather-seated riding breeches that were now terribly stained, the gown would be something clean and fresh, even if just for one night. Though it didn't make sense to buy it, it seemed somehow essential. But a monk couldn't buy a nightgown. Ah, but she was a monk on a hant-marking mission. If asked, she'd say the nightgown was a gift for the wife of the Cumberlandian headman who allowed their mission in his lands. She tucked the rest of the bun in a pocket and resolved to enter, but she stayed where she was, looking at her face's reflection in the window. Had Nan once loved this person, but didn't anymore. The thought made her stomach, though filled with bread, feel empty. She took the bun from her pocket and bit into it as she resolved to go inside.

Funny, it took courage to enter. She was going to fight The Scyon, but hesitated at entering a shop? No, only this kind of shop. She never had occasion to pick a pretty chemise or nightgown for herself. In Sylvania, by the time she'd grown old enough to have such clothing, she simply began to use those left behind by her mother from the drawer her father never opened. At Solace, one was given a plain, coarse undershirt, then tasked with making one to replace it for the storeroom. She wasn't in Sylvania or Solace.

Inside, surrounded by beautiful women's intimate clothes, she felt as out of place as if she were a man, or a child peeking at her mother's things. The shopkeeper, a girl only a few years beyond Jesquin's age, thankfully was tatting lace and seemed determined to keep at it rather than decide what to say to a monk, giving Arvana the leisure to inspect the gown without interrogation. As she touched the finely woven soft cotton of the blue nightgown, she remembered secretly opening the drawer and trying on her mother's lace-trimmed chemises and nightgowns when her father and Allasan were in the barn. Though the sleeves hung far down past her hands and her tiny body was lost in the draping fabric, she envisioned herself as a grown woman, the mysteries of her body tantalizingly only half-hidden by the thin layer of fabric. The blue nightgown wasn't as transparent as her mother's or as frilly with ruffled lace about the sleeves, but it was pretty in its own way. No one would see her in it. She had the coin for her own room. She pointed to the gown and in her deepest voice asked, "How much?"

The shop girl looked up from her tatting. "A quarter crown."

It was a dear price. Perhaps she was meant to haggle the price down, but the less she spoke, the better. So, she nodded and the girl came, took the gown from the window, folded it, wrapped it in a sheet of flower-printed paper.

As she came from the shop, Degarius met her. Through a mouthful of bread, he mumbled something in Gherian. He must have been in the bakery just after her.

"I don't understand."

He swallowed. "I asked why you were in there." Clear disapproval was in his voice.

She peeled back the paper wrapping on the nightgown. A hint of blue showed. "I wanted something clean."

"You'll never use it, unless you want to freeze. It was foolish—"

"It was my coin. I don't need your approval," she said and shoved the package into her coat. "Have you found an inn?"

"We're leaving now." Then quietly, he said, "There are reward fliers plastering the wall by the fruit seller."

The wrapping paper crushed against her chest as she turned and headed to her horse. She was disappointed they had to go, but if staying was imprudent, it was imprudent. Couldn't he have been just a hair kinder, though? That he despised her was clear. But her bucket was already overflowing with his derision. Why must he ladle on more?

When Kieran returned, they rode nonstop through town to the watch house before the tunnel the ancients had cut through the mountain. In the bright afternoon, Verdea Crossing was a hole in the rock-faced mountainside that looked like a gaping, toothless mouth.

"I bought spiritbanes. They're in my pack," Kieran said with a warier eye to the tunnel than the watch house. "The ancients made it, and I've heard

Cumberland is full of unmarked hants. Hold up. Let me get them."

Spiritbanes were useless, Arvana wanted to say, a superstition. The dead couldn't hurt you. But it seemed wrong to speak about the things man shouldn't know. She took the spiritbane Kieran offered, a large one on a leather string. She lifted it to put around her neck, but the pungent smell gagged her and her horse curled its lip in disgust, so she tucked the string into the back of her belt.

At the watch house, the two guards patrolling the tunnel were playing cards. The tunnel shortened the treacherous trip over the mountains from days to a short level ride, though few chose to venture in judging by the guards' boredom. One of the redcoats shook his finger at the other guard then laid down his cards. "Don't look at my cards." To them, he said, "Ah, monks. Stop and get a torch. You'll need it in the tunnel. It's a long, dark ride."

Arvana glanced to the guardhouse. A posting giving the price on Degarius's head was tacked to the door. She had better get the torch.

As she dismounted, a guard asked Kieran, "Why are you going into Cumberland?"

"To mark hants along the road."

"I thought the hant monks wore a full covering."

"Those are in our packs. They are impractical for riding."

The guard nodded. "High time someone marked the hants. I stumbled into a bronze statue there and had bad luck for two years. Good luck with the Cumberlandians, though. They'll commit you to the Maker's peace more likely than thank you. If you can stand the cold, don't light a fire at night. You'll have better luck keeping the robbers off, though you don't look as if you have much to steal."

"Just the hant markers." Kieran reached behind and patted one of his packs, which did contain a bag of the blue glass eyes.

Arvana took a torch from the pile. The second guard, who had a long, dull face and lumpy nose that looked as if it had been broken several times, fanned his cards into a pile. "We won't charge you for it, seeing as how you're going to mark the hants." As she passed him to light the torch, he got up. "You look familiar."

She didn't want to speak and give herself away as a woman, so she merely shrugged as if to say she had no idea why he might think that, and went to remount. He followed her.

Her foot in the stirrup, he said, "I know what it is. Have you been to Shacra Paulus?"

Her pulse raced as she tried to shake her head nonchalantly in the negative. How could he know her?

"I was stationed there on quay duty when they brought Governor Keithan's body from Orlandia.

A Maker's woman played the kithara during the rite. I took note because I play a little myself. Say," he narrowed his eyes at Degarius, "who are you?"

Instinctively, she squeezed her calves to the horse's sides and clucked to the packhorse to go fast. Kieran and Degarius, tight on her tail, galloped after her into the tunnel.

The torchlight grew brighter as they went deeper into the long, dark, tall shaft. The dank smell seemed like the smell of the cold darkness itself, as if it were the thick thing choking out the light instead of a mountain of rock. The hoofbeats echoed eerily until they dashed through a shallow puddle. Then, it sounded as if a whole herd of horses was careening though. Arvana glanced back. A spot of light, like a single star in a vast black night, bobbed up and down. The redcoats were following.

On and on the tunnel went. It seemed like they'd been riding for a dozen minutes. Would the torch last?

Degarius rode up beside her. "Don't look back. It slows you down."

She took a deep breath of stale tasting air through her mouth. Even the bitter scent of the spiritbane would have been more welcome.

The tunnel made a wide turn and grayish daylight lit the rough-hewn walls and then finally eclipsed their torch's golden glow. They rode into the fresh air and blinding daylight. She flung her torch into a rocky ditch and minding Degarius's admonition, crouched well forward on her mount's neck and rode without looking back. The flapping spiritbane tugged at her belt.

※—※—※

Degarius looked back. Kieran was right behind him. The Gherians had come out of the tunnel. Miss Nazar and the packhorse were ahead, racing toward a rickety plank that crossed an eroded streambed. For all love, didn't she see it?

As her horse began the leap, an unbidden image filled the space behind Degarius eyes.

※—※—※

His little group of Frontiersmen were racing from the Gherians who had discovered their confrontation with the creature in Lake Sandela. They were trapped between two pursuing groups and a gully. He shouted for them to cross. Nat, being sentimental, had brought along Micah's horse. "Leave her!" Degarius yelled, but it was too late. They started the jump. They went up, over. They'd cleared the gully. Nat's horse hit hard, throwing him forward. Micah's horse pulled, rolling Nat to the side of his mount. He clung to his horse's neck. But then the horse and rider became one dark tumbling shadow that haunted the air with the eerie joined cries of boy and beast. Ginger,

Micah's horse, veered off from them and disappeared into the close horizon of night.

And Degarius couldn't go back for Nat's body.

⁂

Miss Nazar's horse jumped the creek. It would have been a beautiful thing to watch...but for the packhorse.

She dropped the tether! What a damned fine rider she was. The packhorse landed, and then kept running with Miss Nazar's horse.

Degarius cleared the creek and heard Kieran come over after him, but suddenly the hoofbeats ceased. Kieran had stopped, wheeled his horse around, and was aiming an arrow at the redcoats. Was the fool trying to get himself killed?

The brother let loose an arrow and nocked another as the first arrow hit the front-riding soldier in the shoulder. The second arrow hit the farther back horse in the chest. It stumbled and went down on its knees, throwing the rider. More arrows, with time to be expertly aimed, left Kieran's bow and found their marks. Then, the brother stowed his bow, but didn't turn and ride. What in all hell was he doing? Was he dismounting?

"Kieran!"

⁂

At Degarius's shouting, Arvana stopped. She caught the packhorse's tether and led him to Kieran who was slowly sliding from his horse.

When his feet touched the ground, he crumbled to his knees. Clinging to a stirrup with one hand, his other fumbled with the spiritbane. "It wasn't like taking a deer. Not like it. I killed two men. Maker, how can you forgive me?"

Degarius grasped him under the arm. "You were doing your job. If you love the Maker, get up and ride. Wipe your damn bloody hands on me, if you want. I've killed a hundred men. What are two more?"

Kieran leered at Degarius, but his whole body hardened, and he rose and began to remount.

For a moment, Arvana felt everything she once had for Degarius. He meant what he'd said to Kieran. He bore the ugly trials of this world so others wouldn't have to. A monk, who'd chosen a peaceful life, shouldn't have been called upon to kill. It was why the superior told Degarius about the girl birthing the draeden. She knew his conscience wouldn't abide it.

Her heart went out to Kieran, too. His anger at Degarius had temporarily replaced his grief. It wouldn't last long, though. As well-intentioned as Degarius was, it was impossible to simply wipe the blood from one's hands. She clucked to her horse to move and opened her hands from the reins. They had the blood of Chane Lerouge and a hundred Solacians upon them. The Maker had a special grace for Degarius and Kieran. There wouldn't be one for her. The blood was there by her own mistakes, not out of duty or a sense of justice...until she faced the Gherians. Not that one blood could cleanse the other.

LIFE AND DEATH

Cumberland, six days later

While riding, Degarius slipped a knuckle under his glasses and rubbed the sleep from his eye. What he'd give for a cup of coffee. To avoid drawing attention to themselves, they'd not made a fire since entering Cumberland so the nights were cold and the mornings a coffee-less, frosty headache. But the strategy had worked. No soldiers or robbers had set on them during the night. During the day, the road, more of a narrow, often steep path through the mountains, was quiet except for the sound of their horses kicking through the leaves. By good luck, they'd avoided thieves. Or, if bandits had seen them, they'd had a sliver of compunction at robbing Maker's men.

As Degarius rubbed the other eye, Kieran's blurry figure flagged them to stop. Damn it, it would be his luck to meet bandits after congratulating himself for avoiding them. One hand went to his sword; the other straightened his glasses. Far ahead, a doe was grazing roadside. Had Kieran stopped to watch her? The animal held its head attentive, took a few steps into the brush, and then returned to eating. Degarius relaxed his sword hand.

Kieran dismounted in a slow slide and gave Miss Nazar the reins. He crouched low and stalked the doe with a high-stepping gait. The doe flicked her tail and bounded into the woods. Three other deer previously hidden in the evergreen brush darted across the road. Kieran disappeared after them.

"What's he doing?" Degarius wondered aloud. Kieran hadn't taken his bow. "Does he mean to take it with a knife? I'm not stopping to cook."

A cry, half surprise and half agony, cut through the cacophony of birdcalls.

Silence.

A man's shout, not Kieran's, and the rustle of footsteps in the forest carried through the hush. They were coming nearer.

Degarius drew Assaea.

Miss Nazar was ahead of him with Kieran's horse. A thief in the woods could kill her with an easy shot. "Get off your horse and get behind it," Degarius said. If they tried to ride away now, they'd be shot in the back. And a sword was no good at a distance. Degarius resheathed his sword, dismounted, took his bow, and ducked behind his animal—the only thing Cumberlandians would guess a monk had of value. They wouldn't risk wounding it.

Degarius glanced to Miss Nazar. She was holding the Blue Eye. If she had to use it, the advantage of surprising the Gherians with it was gone, but at least they'd be alive.

A Cumberlandian, clad in simple leather clothes, came from the forest. He wore his bow slung over his back and was supporting a hopping Kieran—a shaft stuck out from his thigh, near his hip. In Anglish, with a drawling Cumberland accent, he said, "I live up the hill. For three years I apprenticed a surgeon in Acadia." Slowly, so as not to appear threatening, he held up an arrow with a brutal-looking three-bladed flared tip. "Without dowels, it's hard to remove and he'll bleed out soon. I meant to kill a deer, not a holy man."

Degarius released the tension on the bowstring and lowered the bow. If the man had wanted to kill them, he wouldn't have bothered to be burdened with Kieran.

❈-❈-❈

Arvana tied the horses to the fence around the Cumberland home while Degarius and the Cumberlandian carried Kieran to the house. Over his shoulder, Degarius called, "Get the tarp." She found it in the pack and then ran to catch up.

A woman, far along with child, stood in the doorway. Four children poured out around her. From the garden, an older girl appeared with her apron sagging with apples. The little ones raced to her.

Her arms full with the tarp as she entered, Arvana brushed the woman's very round stomach. "I'm so sorry."

"Don't worry. The baby kicks a hundred times harder." The woman spoke in a clear Acadian accent. Why was she living here? She returned Arvana's quizzical look, probably guessing straight off that Arvana wasn't a man and wondering why she was dressed as one. She pointed to the back of the house. "The bedroom is there."

The small house was remarkably familiar. Like her home in Sylvania, it was built around a central fireplace and had a loft. A vague sadness overcame Arvana as she glanced back to the woman. A toddler darted to the woman, and she tented her apron over his head. No, it was six children, with one on the way. She tapped the boy on the rear and told him to go outside. He waddled to the door, rose on his tiptoes for the latch, and grunted, but he couldn't reach it. *This could have been my life if I remained in Sylvania*, Arvana thought.

In the bedroom, she unfolded the tarp. It was quick thinking of Degarius to use it to protect the bed. It floated down over the bearskin coverings, stirring a breeze smelling of human scent and old fur.

Kieran groaned as they eased him on it.

The smell, those guttural expressions, brought back a memory Arvana tried never to recall—how her father had suffered at the end. How Allasan couldn't stand it anymore and left. She covered her mouth.

The Cumberlandian unrolled a canvas containing surgeon's instruments. He cut back Kieran's leather breeches.

Blood covered Kieran's leg.

Degarius, who was on the other side of the bed, looked up from Kieran and said to her, "Go outside."

He saw she'd momentarily covered her mouth. He thought her a coward, that she couldn't stand the sight of suffering. He was wrong. "What do you need me to do?" she asked.

"Leave," he said gruffly.

Arvana bunched her fists. This wasn't her fault. "I can help. I've tended worse."

The Cumberlandian, handing a dowel to Degarius said to her, "Go to my wife. She seldom gets visitors."

Fine. Arvana wanted nothing more than to be out of Degarius's proximity. She'd long despised herself for her faults, but never another person except her brother like this. She hated the feeling, but it was so strong she just couldn't tell it to go away. When and how had her guilt over his fate turned into resentment? He was the one who kept coming to the archive, who drew her picture, who wrote the coy letter, who embraced her at Teodor's party, who kissed her in the Citadel woods.

Outside, she found the woman watching the children play leapfrog. Arvana clutched her arms tight and tried to squeeze the anger away so she could find some joy in the children's antics. But when they noticed her, the game disbanded and the little ones ran to hide. The older ones drifted into the orchard.

"They don't know what to make of a lady in breeches," the woman said. "I don't know what to make of one in a monk's cap."

Arvana yanked the cap off, shook out her hair, and gave the answer they'd agreed upon, the one she knew Degarius would give the Cumberlandian if prompted. "The others are monks on their way to Sarapost to start a community. I'm a former sister. When I resigned, my superior let me come with them in order to get home. She thought it safer for me if I dressed as a man."

"Why did you resign?"

Arvana bunched the cap tight in her hands.

"It's none of my business," the woman said, then cupped her hands to her mouth and shouted for the children. One child came hesitantly from behind a rain barrel. Another crept from the door. After darting a few shy glances at Arvana, they started to skip and turn somersaults.

"They're showing off for you," the woman said, half in apology and half in pride.

Arvana managed a smile.

"Don't worry about the monk," the woman said. "My husband will take care of him."

Kieran. Gripped by her bitter concerns, Arvana had forgotten him. She pulled the cap on.

The woman rested her hands on her stomach. "My husband trained in Acadia. It's where I met him. We went along well enough until a neighbor was robbed. Acadians think every Cumberlandian a criminal. They burned our house in retribution. After we barely escaped, he decided to return to Cumberland. It's true it's dangerous here, but even thieves need a doctor now and then so we're left alone."

Outrage simmered in Arvana. The woman was good and kind, and how had this world, both Acadian and Cumberlandian, treated her? How much worse was a draeden? Why bother to save men from it when they were brutal to one another? The Maker may have had a moment of mercy long ago and blessed swords, but what was worth saving now? Men were stupid, never learned. Why was she throwing away her life on what would likely be a futile mission?

"Look," the woman said and laughed. A bump had appeared on her stomach. She covered it with her palm and followed it as it moved.

Arvana's curiosity, and the woman's laughter, eclipsed her anger.

"This one never sleeps. It kicks day and night."

Unconsciously, Arvana put her hand on her own stomach as she watched for another kick. What an odd sensation it would be to have something moving inside.

The woman must have seen her wide-eyed interest. She grasped Arvana's hand and pressed it where hers had been. "Do you feel it?"

A small yet sharp kick poked through the woman's firm belly. Arvana laughed despite herself.

"You have time. You're still young enough."

Arvana drew her hand away. "That's unlikely." Only as the words came out did she realize how tart they sounded, how they made the woman cradle her stomach in her hands and go silent. She was ashamed of the tone of her reply to a woman who was only trying to be kind, who couldn't understand that she had sacrificed that part of herself to the Maker. She'd stayed empty in order to receive a different kind of gift that never came. Arvana summoned a repentant smile and asked,

"When is your baby coming?" It was a question one woman could freely ask another. After all the years in Solace, though, where such questions never needed asking, she felt odd pronouncing it.

The woman seemed not to notice any awkwardness in Arvana's voice. She brightened and said, "Maybe tomorrow, maybe two weeks." She fell into a description of the other births, of the tremendous pain with the first, but how they got easier and easier.

Arvana listened with both the attention due a miracle and a strange gratefulness. No one had ever spoken to her this way. This, this was why she was going to the Forbidden Fortress. So a draeden would never come here. It was the one thing she could give in return.

❈—❈—❈

"I don't think you're ready to ride," Degarius said to Kieran, but he limped to his horse unassisted. The Cumberlandian had done an admirable job removing the arrow, cleaning the wound, dressing it with honey, and stitching it closed, but one night's rest was hardly enough.

"If you can get me on the horse, I can ride," Kieran shot back.

The man could be a stubborn ass. "Fine," said Degarius. He'd spoken his concern. If Kieran insisted on riding, it was his pain to bear. At least they'd be in Sarapost all the sooner. Degarius helped boost him and settle in the saddle.

Miss Nazar, who'd been rummaging in her pack, was heading back toward the house. Why was she going back? They'd said good-bye and thanks. What was that blue thing dangling from her coat?

He followed, but stopped in the doorway. She didn't see him. Her back was to him as she opened her coat and slipped out the blue nightgown.

"I want you to have this," she said to the woman. "It's never been worn. Your husband will like it."

The Cumberlandian held it out by the shoulders. "My husband doesn't need any encouragement."

Both laughed bashfully.

"It's too beautiful. I can't accept it. It's too generous," the woman said with an accepting grin.

"No, not generous at all," Miss Nazar said. "I'll never wear it."

The grin fell from the woman's face.

Miss Nazar went on, "I sleep on the ground. It's cold. This isn't practical for me."

"But you're going home."

"Please just take it," Miss Nazar said.

The Cumberlandian woman clutched the nightgown to her, and then looked past Miss Nazar to him. Her expression asked a question, but what it was, he couldn't guess. The nightgown was Miss Nazar's to do with what she pleased.

"Good luck with the baby," Miss Nazar said. "I hope it's easy for you."

Clutching the nightgown, the woman threw her arms around Miss Nazar, pressing her belly to her. She whispered in Miss Nazar's ear, who nodded in return and said, "Yes, I promise."

When Miss Nazar turned to leave and saw him in the doorway, her pleased look went stony. She swept past without a word.

Degarius closed the door behind them. What was the sour look for? He hadn't told her to give the gown away. "I gave them two crowns. That was enough payment."

She suddenly went as hot-faced as a kettle at boil. "It was a gift. A *gift*," she said as if he didn't understand the meaning of the word. "What is the word in Gherian?"

What the hell? What had his pin been? "I gave you my medal."

"To absolve your conscience—both times." She hooked a foot in the stirrup. "That's not a gift."

He chewed his lip. "And the scroll for you to mourn the governor? I spent a fortune on it."

Her foot dropped from the stirrup to the ground. She crossed her arms over the saddle and buried her face in them. So, this woman thought she could fight The Scyon when she couldn't even keep dry eyes over the truth.

She wasn't going anywhere past Ferne Clyffe.

"Maker help you both," Kieran said and rode between them.

❦ ❦ ❦

Four days later, north Cumberland

Kieran groaned. The low, throaty rattle set Degarius's teeth on edge each time he heard it. Kieran's thigh healed well at first. Then, on the third day, it began to weep copiously and slough gray tissue. Degarius cleaned the wound as best he could, Miss Nazar dressed it, and they'd kept riding. They were, perhaps, only two days from Ferne Clyffe. But yesterday Kieran woke clammy and feverish. By noon, he couldn't sit in the saddle. Degarius had rigged a travois to Kieran's horse's stirrups and towed him since.

Kieran moaned again and muttered for what must have been the hundredth time that afternoon, "I'll never see the Maker. I killed two men."

"Let's stop for lunch and give him another dose of birch bark powder," Degarius said to Miss Nazar. He spotted a small path off the main one. It led to a meadow of brown grass.

They dismounted and each unlashed a pole from a stirrup and eased the travois to the ground. She opened the apothecary box. "There's only one dose left."

"Give it to him."

"The Passage Prayer. Say it for me Hera. Where are you, Hera?"

She froze, the vial in one had, its cork in the other. Kieran's calling her *hera* hadn't escaped her.

"I'm here, Heran Kieran." She mixed the powder in a small draught of water, sat on her heels beside the monk, and held the cup to his lips.

Kieran managed a feeble sip then started muttering again. "Pray the Passage Prayer for me, Hera, before it's too late."

She held the cup to him again. "Heran, it's not come to the Passage Prayer," but she looked to Degarius with a question—had it come to that? Was Kieran going to die?

Degarius wanted to shake his head no, but he'd seen these cases before. The man was certainly delirious, calling Miss Nazar *hera*. And his sense of doom, the surety of death, was a bad sign. Even if they could find a doctor, nothing could be done.

Miss Nazar sat the cup aside, closed her eyes, and began a prayer. Her lips moved, formed every word, but she only gave the slightest, reluctant, breath to them, as if they were a penance to say.

Kieran grew still, so Degarius paced to the far side of the clearing. He'd rather have his knuckles busted than listen to Solacian chanting, even a chant done halfheartedly. Had she ever done it with the whole? But he turned to practical matters. How he was going to bury the man if he died before they reached Ferne Clyffe. They didn't carry a shovel.

"Heran!" Miss Nazar cried.

Degarius spun around. Kieran was on one elbow. His eyes darted wildly. "Where is *he*? I failed. I killed men for nothing. *He* left. *He* took it. I was supposed to make sure he kept his word."

"Kieran, you didn't fail." Miss Nazar grasped the monk's shoulders and pressed him to lie back down. "Lord Degarius is here. He won't take it."

Damn. Why did she have to say those last words with such certainty? Degarius returned to them.

Kieran half-closed his eyes and his head drifted to the side. The birch tea must have started to work. "After I killed the men, I prayed every waking moment, hoping the Maker would forgive me. I prayed for a sign. I thought the deer was my sign. When I was fourteen, when I was good, I touched a doe. I followed her for hours, moved so slowly, cautiously. The surprise in her eyes when she felt my hand...that was the happiest I've ever been. I always thought being with the Maker would be like that happiness."

Degarius ran his fingers through his beard and wished he'd never felt contempt for Kieran. There was something fine about him, about his realizing the worth in an act like touching the doe. It wasn't for glory or gain, but to connect with something beyond self. Degarius wondered what his happiest moment was. Killing the draeden was tainted by the deaths of Nat and Micah and the damage the water had done to his feet.

No, there was nothing happy about that moment.

Winning his first tournament and earning Assaea from his grandmother? That was happy. Reading the letter granting him the generalship made him happy, though he'd always expected to be happier. Those *were* bright spots. But beneath the memories he *wanted* to think his happiest, was the truth. Not a bright, shiny truth. Sometimes the truth, and happiness, was as deep and black as the moment of forsaking oneself before sleep. Kissing her had been that kind of oblivion.

What had been her happiest moment? She seldom spoke of her life before Solace, but he gathered from what the superior said that it was a hardship. She blamed herself for her father's death. He looked back on their acquaintance. The happiest he saw her was when she woke in his arms after she'd fainted before the fire. It was a moment of pure joy. A moment, as Kieran said, uncensored by thought or word, that showed one's true nature.

Kieran, speaking again, drew Degarius from reflection. "I thought the Maker had answered my prayers by sending the doe. If I could touch her, it would be a sign that I was clean again. But instead, *this* happened." His fingers plucked at the spiritbane he wore around his neck. "It doesn't keep them away. The dead soldiers still follow me. I can hear their horses, always hear them."

Kieran turned his face to the sky. His eyes glazed and his whiskers stood out like black barbs from his sickly white skin.

As Degarius swallowed an unexpected surge of pity and repulsion, Kieran reached out, pointed to the overcast sky, whispered, "The doe...there...she's coming," and then collapsed, senseless and limp except for the corners of his mouth that still clung to a smile.

Degarius peered at the sky. It was nothing but a gray sheet. He glanced to Miss Nazar. She hadn't bothered to look. "Your prayer helped him," he said.

She shook her head. "He's going to die."

The dull *thud* of an arrow piercing a tree punctuated the word die.

Degarius drew his sword.

Laughter came from all sides, then one Cumberlandian after another appeared from behind the surrounding trees. There were six in all, with drawn arrows.

Thieves.

"Lockanlo," Miss Nazar cried. She had her hand on the relic, but instead repeated, "Lockanlo."

One the thieves motioned for the rest to stay their arrows. "Don't move. You've trespassed our hant," he said in Anglish. "You owe us spirit money."

Kieran awakened and wildly darted his glazed eyes. "Hant?"

The man who spoke approached. By kicking the grass, he cleared a spot and then pointed to a gray slab of granite. Dirt filled the carved lettering. "These are the graves of our ancestors."

"The spirits will follow us," Kieran cried.

"They are already following you." The Cumberlandian laughed again.

Degarius glanced to the thieves. Why hadn't they killed them? Why in all hell didn't she use the relic? They weren't going to chat all day. He looked to her and grimaced at her chest, but she did nothing. Damn it, if there was any time to use the Blue Eye, it was now.

The Cumberlandian gave an order and two men lowered their bows and went to the horse rigged with the travois. They rummaged through the packs. One found the bag of hant markers and gave it to the headman who spoke Anglish. He then went to untie the travois. They led the horse, with its packs, down the path to the main road.

Were they really going to leave with just one horse?

The Cumberlandian headman took one of the hant markers from the bag, knelt beside Kieran, and put the blue glass eye on the brother's chest. "The spirit money must be paid."

The hant marker rose and fell on Kieran's heaving chest.

"Lockanlo," the Cumberlandian said to Miss Nazar, who was on the other side of Kieran. He then drew a knife and plunged it into the soft spot in Kieran's neck. "May the thirst of the dead be satisfied with this blood."

Now, Nazar, now.

Still, she sat on her heels next to Kieran's bloody body and across from the Cumberlandian as he pulled out the knife. He could stab her in an instant.

Now.

The Cumberlandian leaned forward, but instead of aiming the knife at her, he simply rose. The bloody knife dangling in his hand, he headed down the path with the rest of his party.

Miss Nazar reached into the apothecary's box. The thieves had left it behind. She wadded a bandage and pressed it to Kieran's neck.

"Don't bother."

"I have to. It's making a noise. His breath is coming through the wound."

"What in all hell is *lockanlo?*"

"The thieves' code to tell friend from foe. The woman told it to me."

"Why didn't you tell me?"

"She made me promise to share it with no one. Anglish aren't supposed to know it."

So that was what the woman had whispered to Miss Nazar after receiving the blue nightgown.

Miss Nazar took her hand from the bandage. "He's dead. We should bury him."

"We should leave."

"There's no reason to fear the hant. The dead are everywhere."

"You should fear the living. And, we don't a shovel."

She looked to her hands, as if considering using them to dig. For all love, why would she contemplate such a folly? As much as he hated leaving behind his dead, sometimes it was necessary. "It won't work," he said. "The ground here is too hard, full of stone."

"I know."

TALISMAN

Field Marshall Fassal's house, Sarapost-Gheria battlefront

F assal had dismissed the last of his advisors when Caspar went to the window and began to howl. Then came cheering. It could only be for one thing. His wife had arrived in the border hamlet now serving as the command for the troops. Though her presence must draw him away from duties, he now considered Jesquin, as the cheering suggested, might be a talisman. She'd spark enthusiasm, for who wouldn't love her?

He made a last moment's appraisal of the co-opted house. The parlor was so small the dog could hardly turn about in it without unsetting the small tables. The windows were drafty and the walls shabby despite having been patched and painted. New linens, gold-rimmed plates, and two cartloads of furniture only served as foils to highlight the place's rusticity. Still, the house was the best the hamlet had to offer Sarapost's field marshal and his wife. As a consolation, Fassal thought that though the house might be rustic and uncomfortable, the bed upstairs wasn't. Not that he thought about their sleeping in it.

He did the obligatory hemming and hawing to his staff about preferring to stay in the tent amongst his troops. He knew Degarius, wife or no, would have been in the field sharing his men's hardship. At the remembrance of his friend, Fassal closed his eyes and exhaled heavily. What had happened to Degarius? The redcoats reported that he took the Solacian to Solace and then disappeared. Was he still alive? He'd kill himself before anyone put hands on him to collect the bounty. Had he heard of the terrible fire at Solace? Learning of her tutor's death on the heels of her brother's, and then her father's fury over her secret marriage, had nearly sunk Jesquin. But the one good thing her misery did do was convince her father to acknowledge their marriage and allow Jesquin to go to Sarapost. All seemed well until Fassal had to leave for the front. From Jesquin's increasingly despondent letters, he knew that without him she was slipping into despair and growing homesick for Acadia. His sisters endeavored to entertain her, but they couldn't replace a husband. There was nothing to remedy the homesickness until she proposed joining him. Then her correspondence teemed with excitement. She diverted all the latent energies left from the unrealized grand wedding into arranging a life as the field marshal's wife. And now she was here. Fassal pushed aside the gloominess, and though he told Caspar to stay, the dog followed him outside to meet the coach.

With an escort of smartly outfitted guards and Jesquin waving her gloved hand from the coach window to the cheering soldiers, it was like a small parade. The coach was still rolling when Fassal opened the door. Batting her lashes, Jesquin snuggled into her coat's plush fur collar and asked with tender teasing, "Have you missed me, Gregory? Aren't you going to welcome me?"

How could she be prettier than he remembered?

The coach lurched to a stop. Fassal slipped his hand inside her coat and kissed her. She was everything warm, soft, and reassuring in this blasted camp. "I have a big bed to introduce you to, sweetheart. I'm tired of sharing it with Caspar. He snores."

Jesquin giggled, for the dog had stuck its snorting nose in the coach. "So do you."

LILY GIRL

Near Ferne Clyffe

My land begins here," Degarius had announced a full twenty minutes ago. They were still riding at a fast clip past vast tracts of wood, fallow fields, silos, and pastures dotted with sheep and black cattle. Arvana knew he wasn't a poor man, but she'd never imagined his holdings so large. Several villages must have lived off the working of his land.

They rounded a bend in the road and Degarius slowed and halted at a drive sided by square stone pillars. Perched atop his mount, he was making a survey of the prospect—and what a prospect it was. Though he'd spoken often of his home, she had always pictured it as like one of the nicer farms in Sylvania. It wasn't. Ferne Clyffe was finer, in a way, than the mansions of Acadia. Situated in the wide curve of a river, with gardens to one side and orchards to the other, it seemed a part of the landscape. Even in fall, surrounded by bare trees and a brown expanse of lawn, it was a handsome two-story house with a grand front door, a dozen windows across the front, six dormers in the attic, and a circle drive in front of it all. How would it be in summer, to run barefoot across the swath of green lawn to the river, to have a choice of fruit straight from the trees, to cut an apron full of flowers and still have more for the next day and the next? Far to the right, half-hidden by trees, was a magnificent barn. What her father would have given for such a barn. "It is..." She was going to say *beautiful*, but stopped. At one time, he said it would please her to see Ferne Clyffe. At one time, maybe for just an hour or two, perhaps he'd thought what it would be like for them to live here. Now, hers was the last opinion on earth he'd seek.

"Is that smoke?" Degarius suddenly asked.

Smoke? Draeden? How could it have found them here? Arvana clutched the Blue Eye and scanned the sky. There was no smoke except for the light gray billowing from Ferne Clyffe's chimneys.

"The damn steward is a usurper," Degarius snarled and took off in a gallop.

By the time Arvana understood his concern was over the occupation of his home, he was too far ahead to catch. Without waiting for her, he dismounted, drew his sword, hurtled the steps, and burst through the front door. While Arvana tied the horses, she heard him shout, "Mrs. Karlkin, why is my house open?"

Arvana tiptoed across the porch and peered around the open door. A handsome, stout woman with a halo of blond-going-gray hair was standing in the foyer. She was likely the housekeeper Degarius had been yelling at. With her arms crossed over her apron in satisfaction, she was watching a weeping Chancellor Degarius embrace his son. Through sobs, the chancellor said, "Fassal has made a public condemnation...but issued no call for your arrest...still it's dangerous...the price on your head."

The housekeeper saw Arvana and gave her a head-to-toe look. Feeling like a spy, Arvana was about to retreat to the steps, when the woman motioned her inside with unexpected friendliness.

"I'm at liberty?" Degarius asked his father.

The chancellor released his son and looked at him from arm's length. "Myronan, don't hope for it. They've stripped you of your appointment. As it is, we're lucky King Lerouge didn't pull his troops. Plus, you have no time. The war likely starts in three days. We think the Gherians will declare at the end of their Winter Solemnity. Alenius has called a meeting of the Cabinet of Counties to mark the event—at sunset in the Fortress. The nine days of atonement began a week ago."

"So soon," Degarius muttered. "We'll just make it."

"We? Going where?" The chancellor turned around and narrowed his rheumy, astonished eyes. "Hera Solace?" He glanced to Degarius. "Myronan?"

"Miss Nazar is with me."

His father pinched his brow and looked between them. Undoubtedly, he'd heard from Lady Martise the circumstances of his son's disgrace. Undoubtedly, he would blame her, too. Though he'd been the kindest of men in Acadia, he was Degarius's father. He was probably wondering why she was here when his son so obviously disdained her. Arvana steeled herself for a chilly reception.

Instead, the chancellor said matter-of-factly, "I'd heard you'd perished in Solace with the rest."

With the rest. Why couldn't he have just said something unwelcoming? The rest.

"Mrs. Karlkin," Degarius said, "I need the keys to the attic and my grandfather's chest."

A great ring of keys came from the housekeeper's apron pocket. She singled out two. "These would be them, Lord Degarius."

"The attic?" his father asked. "What must you have from the attic this moment?"

"Something I should have looked for a long time ago," Degarius mumbled as if to himself and started up the stairs. "It would have spared me a world of trouble."

Arvana began to follow when the housekeeper curtsied to her. "Excuse me, but how should I address you? I heard hera and miss."

"Miss, now."

"Ah yes. For now." The housekeeper curtsied again. "Most excellent."

As Arvana grasped the baluster, she turned to give the woman the only thing she could for her kindness—a grateful look. The housekeeper accepted it with a smile so warm it consumed her genial, black, quail-like eyes. Intuitively, Arvana knew all the goodness of the world had been bound up in this woman.

At the end of the second floor hall, Degarius unlocked a door to narrow, steep attic stairs. His father led the way up to a cavernous attic flooded by channels of light coming in through the dormers. It had the fusty smell of a dead person's house that had been kept locked and unswept for many moons. Degarius weaved through crates, past an old table with a baby cradle stacked on top of it, to a big cedar chest.

In Sylvania, her family home didn't have an attic, or the extraneous bits and pieces leftover from life to keep in it. An attic was a strange, cold place, like Hell—full of things not good enough, not necessary, left to themselves. Except one thing here was necessary, just as one soul in Hell had been. Poor Lina. What had she done to deserve damnation? While in Hell, Arvana couldn't ask, and Degarius never seemed surprised, or shaken, to hear of her fate. Lina *had* molded her grandson into a consummate martial man. Perhaps, if not bribed with Assaea, he'd have been content to manage Ferne Clyffe. Dirt, instead of blood, would have stained his hands. Was that enough to damn her?

Degarius grabbed the trunk by one handle and dragged it into the light. Kneeling before it, he inserted the key in the lock and tried to turn it. He jiggled the lock, slid the key in and out again, his face growing redder with each attempt. He hammered the chest with his fist and then turned the key with all his force. The key bent and the lock remained stalwartly closed. With a growl of irritation, he threw down the key and rose to rummage through the mounds of household goods. After considering and rejecting a table leg, he found a sooty fireplace poker. "Move back." He brought the tool down in a perfectly aimed glancing blow against the lock. Nothing. The muscles in his neck stood out and he grimaced as he raised the iron for another strike, then another. Each blow was louder, like the thunder in an approaching storm.

Arvana involuntarily cowered. He was unbelievably strong and persevering. Lina had enticed him to train by offering the sword, but the strength and will were all his. There was no one better to have Assaea. Could she say the same of herself and the Blue Eye?

Crack.

With a heavy exhale, he picked the lock from the mangled wood. It was intact, but the metal rings through which it passed were no longer attached to the chest. He dropped the lock, threw the lid open, and took from the chest a black coat decorated with medals, gold buttons, and lace. "My grandfather's uniform," he said. By the way he caressed the garment, touched the medals, Arvana guessed he was thinking about his own brief generalship.

He passed the coat to her and rummaged deeper in the trunk. He pulled out half-a-dozen books, passed three to his father, and kept the others. She was left holding the mothball-scented uniform.

"These are personal," the chancellor said upon opening one. "I don't see it is our business reading them. Myronan, what is this about?"

With a half-guilty glance to the book in his hand, Degarius said, "Before she died, she told me I should read these. I never had occasion until now."

"It doesn't mean you should read them. You know she wasn't right those last years. She thought you were my father."

"I'm guessing grandfather told her something of the Forbidden Fortress."

"Why do you need to know?"

"The thing I killed in the lake was a draeden, an immature draeden. They have another that I guess they'll unleash on Sarapost at the end of Solemnity. Don't you have any intelligence on it?"

"We know that Sovereign Alenius is planning to unveil something at the end of the Solemnity, but we thought it merely the announcement of their first push into Sarapost. We've heard rumors of something strange to the far north, but a draeden? That's impossible."

"I've seen it," Degarius said. "It was what burned Solace. Our troops don't stand a chance. They'll be dead in minutes. Alenius is going to unveil it and maybe The Scyon. Only The Scyon can raise the draeden."

The chancellor gaped. "You intend to go to the Forbidden Fortress?"

"Where else?"

Clutching the diaries to his chest, the chancellor teetered backward and melted into a threadbare armchair. "If what you say is true, you'd be undertaking a fool's errand. The ancients used blessed swords and a Blue Eye against The Scyon. Our best course is to alert King Fassal and disband all our troops at the front until King Lerouge can bring Artell. But a Blue Eye?"

Arvana caught her breath. Was he going to tell his father everything? As much as she admired the chancellor, he'd been an official. His allegiance was with Sarapost. He shouldn't know.

Sure enough, Degarius said, "The Solacians have been keeping—"

"Degarius," Arvana said firmly and cupped her hand over where the relic lay beneath her coat.

"They've been keeping a Blue Eye ever since Paulus died. Their superior gave it to Miss Nazar."

Arvana knotted her fist beneath his grandfather's uniform. How dare he?

The chancellor nearly dropped the diaries he held. "You?"

If his father was going to know the truth, he might was well know all of it. "I was sent to judge if Prince Lerouge could use the relic. He wasn't the best man, but he seemed to have changed and your son...he can't use it. So, I gave it to the prince."

The chancellor nodded. "Lerouge had Artell, Lukis's sword and an army."

"Grandmother gave me Assaea when I won my first tournament," Degarius said haughtily, obviously spiteful at being cast as second best. "So, it's a fool's errand, but not completely foolish."

"My mother had Assaea?" his father asked. "But how?"

Degarius shrugged. "She never told me. I never really believed it was Assaea until"— he glanced to Arvana, but said— "until I killed the draeden." There wasn't even a flicker of appreciation left in his glance for how she'd saved his sword, and life, at the Citadel.

Eyes glazed with introspection, the chancellor said, "No wonder my mother was so disappointed I refused to take up the sword." The chancellor sighed, focused on the books in his lap, and then opened the top one.

Degarius, too, started to read.

Here she was, purposefully left holding the uniform. She draped it over the chest's edge and to pass time, stepped to the window overlooking the back of the house. The river, edged by a bluff on the far side, flowed parallel to the horizon. He'd spoken of learning to swim there.

"Myronan." The way the chancellor said his son's name meant something was wrong.

Arvana turned from the window.

Degarius took the book from his father. As he read, his mouth first pressed into a thin line, then puckered on the ends, as it he'd tasted something bitter.

The chancellor, doubled over, looked as if he'd had the air knocked out of him. What had Lina written to affect them so?

Degarius was shaking his head in disbelief. "Did you know?" he asked his father.

"No."

"What's the matter?" Arvana asked. "Doesn't it show the way? Is it impossible?"

"It shows the way. It is possible." Degarius snapped the diary closed. "But there must be another way, a better way."

"What do you mean? Another way?"

"A way without you."

Arvana's throat pulsed with rising fury. "This is the other way." She pulled the relic from her shirt. "You promised the superior to do this."

Degarius, with chin thrust out and crossed arms, stepped imposingly close. With the resolute confidence of a man sure of his authority, he set his piercing blue eyes on her. "I only promised your superior to come here. I've done that. Now, I must do what's best for my country and people. Make this easy. Give me the relic. I know you won't kill me to stop me."

The lying bastard! She hardened her gaze and met his. She recalled the vision of him from bonfire night, the man made feeble by being drawn through the Blue Eye. By her actions, she'd made her beloved father suffer; she'd do it to him. "You're right. I won't kill you. But I'll make you wish I had."

"Ari."

"Don't call me that."

"Let my father or me find someone to use the relic."

Him or his father? That was lunacy. Her head buzzed with anger. "Is this about you being the hero? You're no better than Chane with his delusion of being Paulus. He wasn't Paulus, and neither are you. I am. Your grandmother begged *me* to help you."

The chancellor was suddenly beside them, holding his hands between them like a bystander trying to stop a fight. "Please."

Degarius motioned him away. "Lina was crazy."

"Crazy to give you Assaea? You think she judged well in that case. Besides, we have but days! If you were to find someone able to use it, you have no idea how crossing the border between life and death can disturb a mind. Just opening the cover to test your champion will ruin the advantage of surprise, an advantage *my* people died for. We have a chance, however small, if we do this together. Here." Arvana thrust the Blue Eye before his eyes. "If you wish to fail, I can't stop you except by a way that is my equal harm. Whom would I find to take Assaea if I must stop you? As much as I wish I could do this alone, I can't." She jabbed the relic at him. "Take it," she screamed. "Take it!"

Degarius raised a hand but placed it to his forehead. "Don't you understand? I don't want you to have to do this."

"It isn't *your* choice. It never has been *your* choice. You're not the general of this battle."

"Damn it," he cursed under his breath, tossed the diary on the table, and strode toward the stairs.

His heavy stomp down them echoed up through the cavernous roof.

Arvana slipped the chain back over her head. The locket was cold against her heaving chest.

The chancellor picked up the diary and held it to her. "It is *my* mother's, such as she was. If you wish to see it, I consent." He motioned to the armchair.

Arvana accepted the book and the invitation to sit. So much anger had sapped the marrow from her bones.

Lina wrote:

I dread passing this confession to you, Nani. It is a shame I've hidden from everyone except your grandfather. Even he, however, did not know the whole truth of it. Otherwise, how could he have loved me?

The young shouldn't shoulder the errors of the past, but that is often the case in this world. As my excuse, let me tell you I, along with every other country girl, believed being a Lily Girl was our chance to become accomplished and serve the Sovereign Alenius. We heard that he was the most handsome of men and that he would take the most beautiful, talented girl in Gheria to be his wife. My father wished me to marry Stellan, but then he was but the second son of a neighboring lord. I thought I deserved better. So, when the eunuchs came for Lily Girls, I slipped away to the village.

I meticulously studied every art in which the eunuchs and old Lilies schooled us. I enjoyed when they rubbed my skin with oil, powdered my face, and fitted me with the finest dresses.

The Sovereign was indeed handsome, but was as vain and impotent as he was beautiful and it made him cruel. He forced me to do unspeakable things to try to please him. I did them, all along hoping that he would make me his wife. For a time, I was the most envied of the Lily Girls. Sapphires were braided into my hair and I wore the best, sheerest gowns. I imagined the day I would leave the confines of a Lily and take my place before all eyes as the queen of High Gheria. But I never conceived Alenius's child, and he grew tired of me. Among the Lily Girls, I fell from the most envied to the most pitied. Then I realized I would grow old, ugly and forgotten within the walls of the Forbidden Fortress. Even being a country lord's wife was a far better fate. I wanted to go home. I begged the clerics, but they only beat me for the audacity of asking. I'm ashamed of what I thought worth my release.

It was found in the most commonplace way. When I was a child, my father ordered a new barn. The workers digging the footings unearthed a trove of artifacts—a broken headstone, a casket containing a man's skeleton whose bony hands locked around a sword hilt, and oddest of all, an immense collapsed rib cage. Inside the rib cage was a clear-shelled egg-shaped object filled with green wafers and silver wires.

Upon piecing together the headstone, my father found it was the marker of Paulus Lerouge's lost grave. Now you know I told you the truth when I said your sword was Assaea.

My father believed the other thing found, the odd egg, was the Beckoner. It was said Paulus's body was buried over The Scyon's. Perhaps the ancients, having lost so much knowledge in those dark times, didn't know how The Scyon was raised. Perhaps they didn't know that there was anything inside the rib cage.

Judging the find too dangerous to reveal, my father had the footings filled and the barn built elsewhere. He reburied the creature, the Beckoner, and Paulus. The sword, however, he kept. He said it was a good thing. I didn't bribe the Sovereign Alenius with the good thing. I wanted my father to be able to keep it. I thought the Beckoner couldn't possibly work after so long, but that the Sovereign Alenius would like to have it as a rare artifact, would accept it as a bribe for my release.

He did want it. He sent me home to get it.

No man is supposed to look upon a Lily Girl unless the sovereign elevates her to a wife. We came and went from his chambers by an underground passage. On the day I left for home, the eunuch led me far into the tunnels. I always guessed they connected more than our compound and the Sovereign Alenius's chamber. Although blindfolded, I remember we turned right only once. We climbed a stairway and came out in a room full of vestments. Here the eunuch removed the cover from my eyes. Leading a blindfolded girl through the Worship

Hall would have aroused suspicion. I remember a dove window above the vestment room's door.

Guards took me home. If I couldn't produce the Beckoner, they would return me to the Forbidden Fortress.

Upon seeing the look on my father's face when I told him my dealings, I changed my mind. I had disobeyed him not only once in refusing to marry Stellan, but a second time by revealing our family's secret. I told the guards I had made the whole thing up because I was homesick and needed to see my family just once. My father corroborated my story. They nearly believed us until a foreman hoping for a reward led them to the site. They killed my father for his deceit. To punish me, they executed the rest of my family. To keep the Sovereign Alenius's word, they gave me my freedom. So you see why, all my life, I have despised the Sovereign Alenius with all my being.

"*You know the truth about the rest of my life. When the War of the Borderlands began, I aided the persecuted Mora Gherians who allied with Sarapost. The Janfa Gherian Clan was within a mile of my home when your grandfather Stellan bravely led a regiment in a desperate stand on the northern quarter of my land. Finally, I saw what a noble man he was. His victory was the beginning of better days. I told Stellan I preferred him to even the emperor and had tried to escape the Forbidden Fortress only because of him.*

I always worried the Gherians will learn to use the Beckoner. I have prepared you as best I can if the worst comes. In the next pages are notes of all I remember of the Forbidden Fortress. It may fall to you, Nani, to avenge me on Alenius.

OF THIS PLACE

Mrs. Karlkin ushered Arvana to a hot bath. A towel and neatly folded chemise waited on a stand. "You were in the attic so long I thought the water would get cold," the housekeeper said.

Arvana wondered if the woman heard her shouting and threats. Perhaps not, since she was being kind. Or she had heard and was being kinder still, knowing warm water would help release the knotty discomfort of anger. Would it help the sick feeling in her stomach from reading the diary and understanding how Lina had damned herself? Even in Hell, Lina formed herself as a Lily Girl, a Lily Girl craving the glory of the throne. She clung to vanity, to the desire to be noticed above all others, though it had caused so much pain. The irony was that in Hell, she became what she desired, but there was no one to notice.

Mrs. Karlkin handed Arvana the soap. "Call for me when you're finished." With a critical eye to the grimy monk's tunic and riding breeches, she said, "I'll find you something to wear to dinner."

As awful as it would be to put back on her filthy clothes, she couldn't impose on the woman. "I have another tunic in my pack."

"I've served in this house as child and woman. You can't appear at the table in the clothes you brought unless you eat with the stable hands, and I'm sure Lord Degarius would never countenance such a thing. We may live far afield in the country, but we keep civilized ways. I'll find a proper dress." She frowned at Arvana's boots. "The slippers might be harder."

Arvana thought to disagree with what Lord Degarius would countenance and assert her preference of eating with the stable hands, but Mrs. Karlkin was bustling away.

The proper dress, in Mrs. Karlkin's judgment, was a crimson bodice and matching skirt. The slippers were a tad long, but a wad of tissue in the toes made them wearable.

"I don't feel right wearing it," Arvana confided as the housekeeper finished repositioning a button so the skirt's waistband fit.

"Nonsense. It's nearly the right size. There's a whole closet and two wardrobes of Lady Degarius's clothes. She always wore lovely things, but a little young for her age. She never reconciled with getting old. I kept thinking her clothes should have gone to the servants long ago to be made into holiday dresses for the children, but fate has a reason for things." Putting her hands to her hips, she made a final appraisal. "It's not in style, but it's lovely on you. Anything would be, though."

With deep reservation, Arvana looked into the full-length mirror. She had never worn a tightly fitted bodice and flowing skirt. She had gone from a Sylvanian girl's leggings and tunic to a Solacian habit. Lina's dress was a real woman's robe, not made to be sensible, but becoming. The image of a fine woman stared back at Arvana. She felt like she knew this woman, but only vaguely, and here they were staring at each other. It was awkward, yet strangely compulsive. She could have stared a long while at this woman, at the gentle slope of her shoulders, at the way her chest rose and fell within the confines of the tight bodice, except the housekeeper summoned her.

"Come along. They'll be waiting. Lord Degarius likes an early dinner."

Mrs. Karlkin did know *that* about her master.

Arvana peeked into the rooms they passed. Every window seemed to open to a worthy view. The furniture was sturdy, yet elegant. But the place didn't seem like *his*. Nothing had probably moved or been changed since Lina had died. They turned into the picture gallery. Mrs. Karlkin paused before a man and woman's portraits that hung side by side.

Arvana recognized Lina. The man had to be her husband Stellan. His hair was blond, like Degarius's, and their beards were the same red. How hadn't Lina thought Stellan grand from the start?

"The General and Lady Degarius's marriage portraits. Behind you," Mrs. Karlkin pointed to two smaller pictures, "is the chancellor as a boy. The other is my master at age eighteen."

It was Degarius half a lifetime ago. His face was thinner, fresher, but the portrait's eyes had the same resoluteness. The artist had captured their sky-blue color perfectly.

"A handsome boy. But he's a handsomer man, don't you think?" asked Mrs. Karlkin.

"Y-yes."

"It's time he had a new portrait made, one befitting the master of this house. Perhaps when he marries. The Maker knows I thought it would never happen and this place would fall into his cousin's hands. But now—such a story—fighting a prince. I know my master. He'd never do it except for the best of reasons. Many a woman in Sarapost wishes herself in your place."

So this was the cause of the fuss. Mrs. Karlkin didn't know her master half as well as she thought. *No woman in Sarapost, or anyplace else, would wish herself in my place.*

-⚜-⚜-⚜-

"Most of the Sarapostan and Acadian units are camped by the headwaters of the Odis River," Degarius's father said. "A dozen Gherian units, under the command of Alenius's brother, are on the other side."

"Is Prince Fassal on the front?" Degarius asked. He rubbed his clean-shaven face. It was amazingly good to be rid of the beard.

"He's field marshal."

"Field marshal?" Out the dining room windows, the dry grassy expanse was glowing golden in the sunset. Degarius pictured himself a general and the draeden swooping down upon his formations. Fassal would be in that exact position if they did not succeed at the Forbidden Fortress. Thinking aloud, he said, "I need one of the elders to give me a clan mark."

"Thorwold can. May I suggest taking the coach and traveling as a cabinetman to the Worship Hall for the Winter Solemnity? You won't be suspected."

"A cabinetman?" He was about to make a snide remark about pasty, bald government men, when he remembered that his father was one, and Miss Nazar, in a red dress, appeared in the dining room doorway. His chest lurched into his throat, and his breeches stretched uncomfortably tight. Damn, what was that about? He wasn't a boy without self-control. How in the hell was he supposed to stand

and pull out her chair? "Did Mrs. Karlkin give you the dress?"

She took a step backward. "I'll change into my riding gear. It makes no difference to me."

Damn her. He hadn't meant it that way. He could care less if she wore one of Lina's old dresses. Mrs. Karlkin was a good manager upon whom he could depend to arrange such things, but—he looked at his own starched, immaculate cuffs—he should have given the order. That was all.

His father, thankfully, rose, pulled a chair out for her and said of her resolve to change, "Do no such thing. Knowing what you propose to undertake, my mother would be pleased."

As Miss Nazar sat, the bodice of her dress gaped open. How could the last thing on earth he needed to think about be the first thing on his mind? He looked adamantly to his father and asked in reference to the command of the division he was to have had, "Who has the third?"

"Reisten was made general," his father replied.

The servers began to bring out dinner.

"I'm astonished by his appointment," Degarius said. "He has few connections and is competent. Was he your recommendation?"

"I can't take the credit. I had already resigned." Of Miss Nazar, he asked, "Would you care for wine?"

"Yes."

Degarius avoided looking at her as he poured the wine. *That* trap wouldn't waylay him again. "You should go back to Sarapost," he said to his father. "Fassal will need you."

"No, I served my time. If you worry about my intrusion into your home—"

"You will stay here as long as you wish." It was reassuring to Degarius that if he didn't return, the land would be in the immediate family's possession a while longer before transferring to a second cousin.

"I couldn't wait to get away from Ferne Clyffe," his father said. "You could never wait to come. Lina left it in the right hands. The place deserved someone who'd care for it properly."

He wouldn't say his father was right, but he was. Though his father had grown up here, he had no notion of how it ran. Degarius poured himself another glass of wine, one to go with the roast pork with apples. It seemed forever since he'd had a decent bottle and real, honest food, most of it from his own land. He'd been away so long he'd forgotten the pleasure of sitting at the head of his own table and having everything as *he* pleased. "Bring another bottle of wine," he called to the steward.

After dinner, his father fell into recounting the anecdotes he'd accumulated from years of meeting nearly every noble in the region. Miss Nazar was an attentive audience. Maybe the stories were interesting. Degarius had heard them so many times he couldn't tell. It didn't matter, though. His father was happy. Degarius pushed the thought to the back of his mind that he might never share such a meal with him again.

The servant coming in to light the candles took him aback. The evening had passed to night, but he was not in the least tired or eager for it to end. His father had grown animated with drink and was telling about how he'd rescued a young Lady Martise from an overturned buggy. "She was a wild driver, still likes a fast two-wheeler..."

Ari smiled as she used to.

Degarius detached himself from the current story; he had heard it a dozen times. Glass in hand, he leaned his weight far back into the chair and found himself suspended in one of those rare moments in which one was acutely aware of the beauty of ordinary life. Was it the effect of the wine? It distilled the raw taste of life into something more potent, yet paradoxically more soothing, than the original fruit. Was it the pleasure of presiding at his table? Or was it the simple relief in knowing the course of his next days? And Ari, he couldn't help but look at her. The chair, the room, the whole of the house seemed somehow connected to her as if she'd always been a part of this place, of his life. His head throbbed. How had everything gone wrong?

"Steward," he called, and whispered instructions.

A short while later, the man brought the bottle. Degarius decanted three glasses of brandy. He'd had the same vintage at Sarapost House in Shacra Paulus. He held the glass to his nose. The floral smell blossomed. With one sip, warmth filled his mouth. He thought of Fassal's slobbering dog, of the pinging hammers in Teodor's shop, of how the sea lapping one's feet could banish the hottest afternoon. He recalled Ari's battle to keep her hem modestly above the water while trying to enjoy the beach with childlike wonder. His heart beat harder as he remembered how it felt to hold her against his chest. To kiss her. "It's funny," he said, "when I drank this in Acadia it made me think of home. Now, it brings to mind Acadia."

"Then it must have an unpleasant finish," Ari said and pushing her glass away, bid them good night in Gherian.

"You're not done with your brandy," his father said.

"It's quite excellent, but I believe I have had too much to drink already."

The glow in Degarius's head vanished. He was suddenly sober. He wouldn't attempt to detain her. Flush in the contentment of being home, he had ventured too near pointless sentimentality. It was really the product of the vineyard. Animosity, which was for the best, came back in all its original vigor. She was beautiful. So what. Thousands of other women were beautiful. He remembered exactly why things went wrong between them.

He was glad when his father lit a pipe. Besides an appreciation of good wine, the occasional indulgence in altartish was the other thing they had in common. "At least one could get exceptional altartish in Acadia," Degarius said.

"Acadia." His father sighed and passed the pipe. "One thing has been bothering me. I should have warned you about Hera Solace and Prince Lerouge. But I guessed you would take exception to my meddling. Lady Martise wrote to me she suspected an attachment on both your parts."

Degarius exhaled a stream of altartish. "I assure you there was none on mine."

His father seemed not to hear through the veil of smoke between them. "I could have told you to be careful of Lerouge, but Lady Martise thought him over it."

"He could've had her," Degarius said with an offhand smirk.

His father put down the pipe and winced. "Have her? Lady Martise and I were at Summercrest this spring when she refused him. He lost his sense and beat her. Not a slap across the face, Myronan. He was brutal."

Degarius dipped a fingertip into the melted candle wax. "Refused him? That is impossible."

When the story penetrated his altartish-thickened skull and nearly held convictions of her impiety, Degarius fixed his bleary vision on the chair where she had sat. She'd not sought Lerouge. She'd refused him, refused to be queen of Acadia. A fierce heat flooded from Degarius's chest into his hands. How could he have doubted her? How? And that bastard Lerouge had laid his hands on her. Hurt Ari. She should have told him. No, of course she wouldn't have told him. She was proud. And there were things they couldn't say to each other. He wanted to crush or throw something, anything to get rid of the pressure centered in his knuckles. The brandy bottle or a chair? Not with his father in the room. He directed all his energy into keeping his hands rigid, tensioning them like set trap springs.

"I should have told you," his father said. "If you had known, you would never have run afoul of Lerouge. This lot wouldn't have fallen to the two of you."

"If I had known..." Degarius's voice broke. "I wouldn't have regretted killing him."

"You should go upstairs, talk to her."

Talk to her? It would be as pointless as trying to make peace with the Gherians. She hated him because he'd given her every reason in the world to. Could he respect her if she did forgive him? He'd chosen to flame his anger over the generalship instead of believe her. He remembered the pleading look in her eyes as she told him she never loved Lerouge. How could she forgive him for choosing anger over faith in her?

Talk to her? His father had no idea of how cruel he'd been in matters big and small. He'd vehemently denied loving her. Those words seemed like fair retribution for his loss. But she was innocent. How did they seem to her? Cruel. He was no better than that bastard Lerouge. Then, he'd upbraided her for buying the nightgown and she'd given it away without hope of ever wearing it. She'd only wanted to be womanly, even if only in the privacy of the night. Ari's only fault was that she'd loved Nan Degarius—a love that cost her greatly. She'd given the Blue Eye to Lerouge. Now, she was entangled in a plan that would likely demand a sacrifice of her he couldn't even name. And when she prayed for Kieran, it had sounded hollow, as if she had no faith in goodness anymore. Damn it, he'd meant it in the attic when he told her he didn't want her to have to go to the Forbidden Fortress. What honorable man could ask it of a woman? And there was no way in hell he could let the woman he loved do it. If he went upstairs and by some miracle she forgave him....

An unbidden image coalesced from the gray fog of regret that sat so heavy on the fore of his mind. In her blue nightgown, she was in his bed. He knelt astride her knees. His hand smoothed upward along her thigh and over her hip, drawing the gown up with it. So lovely. There were innumerable beautiful women in the world, but he hadn't wanted them in the same way he wanted her. He wanted to be gentle, to please her in the most open and most vulnerable act—a man and woman giving themselves to each other. He'd never wanted to love anyone like that before. It had always been about lust, relief, or simple opportunity. He would lean forward, sweep his hair across her stomach and breasts, then go closer and kiss....

No. None of those things could happen. If they did, it would be utterly unbearable going with her to Gheria. Some men were braver going into a fight knowing they had everything to lose. His bravery was of a different sort. Things had to remain as they were. Animosity was for the best. Otherwise, how could he wholeheartedly fight The Scyon or the draeden? So many people, not just the Sarapostan troops, depended on *them*.

Degarius unclenched his hands, took the brandy bottle, and poured another drink for his father and himself. As he sat down the bottle he said, "Swear to me that if I don't return, you'll give her the funds held in my name in Sarapost. She has nothing."

MORE RELICS

I t was time to leave. From her bedroom, which overlooked the front lawn, Arvana watched the coach and four pull around. If she'd been Degarius, she'd never have left this place. But then again, she'd never have left Sylvania, or Solace, had she any choice. A fierce cold wind, which had blown in during the night, whistled through the cracks in the window casing and whipped the horses' manes and tails. She'd need the fur coat and hat Mrs. Karlkin had unhappily laid on the bed. Arvana wanted to tell the woman she'd have just as little pleasure wearing it. It was a gorgeous coat, all of red fox fur. Her mother's coat had only a velvet collar, and she had thought it the finest thing in the world. She'd wanted to look grown-up, to look beautiful.

※ ※ ※

On the morning of the day when everything changed, she begged her father to override Allasan's objection to her going on the sleigh ride. "I'll finish my chores when I get back."

Her father tapped his coffee cup lightly.

Arvana paused with her mug at her lips. *Maker, please let him say yes.*

"Let Ari go," her father said. "With the snow, I can't work on the pasture fence. Stable chores will give me something to do."

"But then there won't be room for one of my friends." Allasan's fist thumped the table.

As if his blind eyes could still see, her father turned his face toward Allasan. "You can take turns riding," he said with a finality that meant another contrary word and no one would be sleighing.

"Fine." Allasan pushed away his coffee without taking a drink.

Arvana scrambled up the loft ladder. She unbound her ponytail and ran her fingers through her hair to separate the waves. No, she wouldn't wear a cap and spoil it. She opened her chest and took out the coat with the velvet collar.

When she came down, she stood at her father's side at the table. "I'm wearing Mama's coat. Do you want to see?"

He rose and ran his hands up the sleeves and over her shoulders to the velvet collar. "I always liked that collar." He smiled, but it was a half-happy nostalgic smile. "I can never believe you're so tall." His fingers lightly touched down the length of her hair. "And your hair is so long. That's nice." He patted the collar once more.

❀ ❀ ❀

"I don't see why you're leaving just as you've gotten here," said Mrs. Karlkin, as she came to Arvana's side. She carried a blue silk-covered case with a pair of gloves atop it. Her usual smile was absent. "I found these gloves for you," she said and laid the gloves beside the coat. Amazingly supple and soft-looking, they had to be kid leather. She handed Arvana the silk-covered box. Inside was a gold ring set with a green gem and collar-style double-strand pearl necklace with a pendant that matched the ring.

"Lord Degarius asked me to give these to you to wear so you look like a lady," Mrs. Karlkin said of the jewels. There was an apologetic tone in her voice, as if she regretted having to fulfill her master's bidding.

Arvana knew full well why he hadn't given them himself, had sent the jewels with Mrs. Karlkin. He didn't want her to mistake the gesture. Of course, he'd sent them as a matter of necessity. They were to be brother and sister traveling to the Winter Solemnity. With a handsome coach and fine clothes, he was obviously a man of great means. It would appear strange if she didn't exhibit the same degree of wealth. And what wealth! The pearls alone were expensive, and if the gems were emeralds it would be worth a fortune. She held up the necklace. "Are the gems real?"

"I'm certain they are."

Necessity or not, thinking aloud, Arvana said, "I'd rather not wear them." They were a sad reminder of Lina's fate and the trap of vanity.

Mrs. Karlkin put a hand to her breast and bowed. "Beg pardon, I understand none of this. I'm only doing as ordered. He's my master."

"Yes, forgive me." It was wrong to put Mrs. Karlkin, who'd been nothing but kindness, in the middle of their bitterness. Arvana brought the ends of the necklace to the back of her neck and fidgeted with the clasp. It was tricky, wouldn't close properly.

"Let me help," Mrs. Karlkin said.

Arvana gave over the necklace and held up her hair so Mrs. Karlkin could fasten it. The Blue Eye gazed up from between her breasts—the housekeeper was removing it. Arvana cupped her hand over the locket. "I must leave it on."

"But it spoils the look."

"I know, but it's a personal heirloom. I always wear it."

The response satisfied the housekeeper. "Does the ring fit?"

Arvana took it, glanced between her hands, and then despised herself for even a second of indecision. She was to wear it on her right hand, not on the hand closest to her heart, the hand on which she'd worn the Solacian silver novitiate's ring. With a slight twist at her knuckle, it was on, but it felt odd, as did the necklace. The finery, like the revealing dress, didn't belong on her. She was like a little girl secretly trying on her mother's things. Not *her* mother's things. Her mother never had anything remotely as elegant—not even that coat with the velvet collar. Arvana took Lina's fur hat. It had a deep crown. When she placed it on her head, the rolled brim of fur came down to her eyes and was soft against her cheeks.

The housekeeper held the coat out and Arvana slipped into it. "It fits well. You're much the same height as the mistress. She never wore it much. Her mind failed that last winter, and we had to keep her close."

"Keep her close?" Arvana put the gloves in the coat pocket.

"She took to thinking my master, Lord Degarius, was her husband, Stellan. If we didn't lock her in her room at night, she went banging on his door and crying that he didn't love her. Why didn't he kiss her? If he went out to ride, she thought him going away to war, and she'd run out into the snow in her stocking feet after him. We had to keep her close."

Arvana felt even stranger wearing Lina's things. What a raw reminder seeing her in them must be to Degarius, just as the memories were for her that the coat had triggered. She regretted her bitterness to him at dinner last night over her misunderstanding of his reaction to Lina's dress.

"Anyway, I suppose they'll be waiting for you, Miss."

Degarius's father was entering the foyer as Arvana descended the last step. He stopped where he was and gazed at her open coat, at the necklace, then explicitly at her hand. A melancholy expression creased the corners of his eyes.

Every bit of common sense had told Arvana not to wear Lina's jewels. It pained her to wear them and him to see them on her. She began to wrench the ring off. "It must be your mother's."

"Lord Degarius told me to give them to her," Mrs. Karlkin chimed. The good woman, who turned deep red from the impropriety of her interjection, curtsied to the chancellor.

The ring was almost off, but his father held up his hand. "They weren't Lina's. They were my wife's, my engagement gift to her."

"I didn't know. I wouldn't have dreamed of...please, take them." Arvana held out the ring. Mortification burned her eyes.

He took the ring. "I gave these things to Myronan as keepsakes. They're his to do with as he pleases." He tilted the ring back and forth, making the jewels flash and a happy, yet nostalgic, expression waxed over him. He looked up, smiled kindly, and held it out to her.

"I can't."

"He gave them well."

Arvana took the ring. She had no choice. But his father was wrong. Degarius hadn't given them to her. They were a necessity. That's why he sent them via Mrs. Karlkin, so there'd be no mistaking his intention. But if just a necessity, why hadn't he given her something less dear?

"I'll see you out," his father said. "The coach is ready."

Degarius was waiting at the coach door. He didn't even glance to the necklace or ring. How could they mean so little to him? He went straight to shaking his father's hand.

She put on the gloves.

"Have a good journey," his father said.

"I will if it doesn't snow. That'll be my damned luck."

That was all they said in parting. That it might be the last time they would see each other was impossible to admit. Arvana knew the feeling. She'd never allowed herself to say good-bye to her father. Even at his last breath, she thought there would be one more.

"Let's go," Degarius said and to her surprise, held out his gloved hand to assist her into the coach. Even through the leather of both their gloves, she felt his thumb find the ring. Why did her heart jump into her throat?

As they turned the circular drive, Degarius looked back at his father, home, and land. No overt emotion showed on his face, but if he was anything like her, she knew he was certainly saying things in his mind to his father that he hadn't said aloud. She pulled off her gloves, glanced at the ring and guessed he hadn't looked at it because it meant nothing; he hadn't looked at it because it meant so much. Sometimes the things closest to the heart were the hardest to acknowledge. He had loved Lina, despite her faults. It was why he couldn't speak of what had happened their last winter together. He loved his mother, too. These beautiful jewels were the remembrances he was taking with him. That was why he made sure she wore them.

What would she have liked to bring? The kithara? Her father's coffee cup? Her mother's coat? Her only mementos of the past were the Blue Eye and the man sitting across from her.

❦ ❦ ❦

Gheria, later that day

Arvana turned the page of her book. They were both reading. Degarius had smartly stashed several volumes beneath the seats. It was difficult reading in the coach, but at least it was something to do. In Acadia, they had read almost every day. It was something they did to be together. Now, it was something they did to be apart.

The coach slowed and came to a stop. She put the book down. They couldn't be there yet. Degarius said it would be a full day of travel, and it was only midafternoon. He, too, had put down his book and was looking out the window.

Regiment after regiment and their supply trains were on the march. The road, crawling with blue-coated men, looked like a brightly colored serpent slithering from one horizon to the other. The notion of impending war hadn't seemed real until that point. They'd traveled all morning zigzagging country lanes, crossing into Gheria on a route so backwoods that it wasn't guarded. Gheria seemed a peaceful place, empty place. Now she understood why. Every able man was being rallied to war.

"That's the main road to the front from the east," Degarius said. "They're sending nearly all their troops there so we'll mass ours to counter. It'll make short work for the draeden."

There were so many men. An endless number of men. Even if they did defeat The Scyon and the draeden, what was to stop the fighting? There would still be a war. The thought hadn't occurred to her before. Killing The Scyon and the draeden averted one catastrophe, a far more widespread one. But not a war. "If we do stop *them*, will Sarapost hold?"

"Many of these men look like new recruits. But so are ours." Degarius didn't sound optimistic.

From the window, Arvana saw a Gherian riding up to the carriage. He began to dismount.

Degarius saw, too. He scowled and opened the coach door.

"The commander wishes to speak with you, sir," the rider said, then added something that Arvana didn't understand.

In Gherian, Degarius said to her, "Stay here," and closed the coach door.

What could they want? Arvana edged to the door to watch. The soldier accompanied Degarius to a mounted weathered man, a veteran commander by the looks of his heavily decorated uniform. What if he recognized Degarius? Arvana removed her gloves and poised her thumb above the Blue Eye's latch.

The general gave Degarius a suspicious once-over, and as he spoke, his face grew animated and angry. Degarius opened his coat and rested a hand on his hip, ready to draw his sword.

Suddenly the general looked to the coach—to her. Degarius shook his head. What was he telling the general *no* about her? The commander held up his hand and Degarius turned and began to walk toward the coach. Degarius waved to her. What did he mean by waving?

The commander dismounted while his escort kept a keen watch on Degarius.

Degarius opened the door, looked over his glasses at her, and said, "The general wants to ask my wife something."

"Well, you better go find her," Arvana whispered. Was he out of his mind? She didn't know Gherian well enough to speak like a native. And to a general!

"Relax." He took her hand from the Blue Eye and guided it to her thigh. He laid his own over it. "I told him you only speak a little Gherian."

Arvana began to rise from her seat to get out when the general motioned her to stay inside. Degarius elbowed the coach door open wider to make space for the general, but kept his hand firmly over hers.

The general's eyes were tired yet filled with earnestness as he spoke slowly and used simple words so Arvana would understand. She couldn't catch everything, but the gist was, "Your husband says you are a good woman, a praying woman. You are going to the Solemnity. At the Worship Hall, pray for my son, Jan. He is ill, can't fight."

Pray for the enemy. Arvana gave what she hoped was a sympathetic-looking smile. In Gherian she said, "I'm happy to pray for Jan."

The general nodded gratefully at hearing his son's name.

Degarius gripped her hand and squeezed it. She'd spoken well enough, perhaps looked pious enough to satisfy the commander that her prayers were worth the trouble of requesting them.

"Pray in Gherian," the general added. "The Eternal Master hears it better."

"I will." Had that been her problem all along, praying in Anglish?

The general gave Degarius an amiable slap to the back and said something about her. She caught *heathen*, what the Gherians called all non-clansmen, and the word *war*. Finally, the two exchanged salutes and Degarius climbed in and closed the door. The moment he saw the commander gallop away, he tore his hat off and flung it on the seat.

"What's wrong? Aren't we free to go? He didn't recognize you, did he?"

"Recognize me? You know what he took me for? Without even a word from me, he took me for one of Sovereign Alenius's cabinetmen going to the Forbidden Fortress for the meeting. They're having a grand dinner. A damn courtier chasing after Alenius's favors. I dared not disoblige him of that notion, so he ranted to me that Alenius is going to award every soldier a parcel of Sarapostan land and pressed me to promise to speak against it. Landowners, like the general, have first lent their tenants as foot soldiers and next will lose them if they get their own holdings in the south. Just the rumor of the reward has brought every man and boy out to fight. Whether or not it proves true makes no difference. They're carrying their hoes to war, ready to break Sarapostan land. Their ranks are going to be twice as big as anyone in Sarapost imagined."

That was terrible news.

"I was thinking, put that ring on the other hand," Degarius said matter-of-factly.

Arvana glanced at her hands. She'd been unconsciously wringing them.

"I don't want any entangling questions. No one would think you're my sister. Your Gherian isn't good enough. It's just lucky the general assumed..."

Her fingers cold, the ring came off without trouble. He blatantly turned to look out the window when she eased it on the other finger. What, did he think she wanted it on *that* finger? She sank into the seat. As she centered the emerald to her finger, she asked, "What did the general say before he left? Did he call me a heathen?"

Still looking out the window, Degarius cracked a smile that Arvana saw in profile. "He congratulated me on bringing a heathen woman to the faith. He said if they were all good like you, we wouldn't need to war. That's rich on many levels."

"That I'm good?"

His smile contracted. "I meant the notion that love trumps war and that anyone could think I brought you to faith."

She wanted to say that whatever faith she'd had must have been of poor quality. It seemed something separate from her, like a coat she wore when she was cold, or the habit she'd left behind at Solace. And to think she once aspired to be a shacra. That would have been yet another costume. Not the real Ari.

The coach pitched forward as the driver sped through a gap in the troop line.

She put back on her gloves. They were on the road north. Tonight they'd stop at an inn, and tomorrow, for the Solemnity, arrive at the Forbidden Fortress. None of this would matter anymore. "Perhaps no one will notice us, and we won't have to pretend anything or even sneak through the tunnels. We can go to the cabinetmen's dinner."

ONE ROOM

Gherian Inn, that evening

Degarius stopped a serving girl carrying a bowl of steaming potatoes that smelled of dill into the dining room crowded with bald-headed cabinetmen and old couples probably bound for the Winter Solemnity. "Where's the innkeeper?"

"Behind you, sir."

"Let me take your coat, madam," the indicated man said to Miss Nazar. Though frazzled, he had the look of an incurably jovial man. To Degarius he said, "It's your lucky night. I have one room left."

It was lucky. They'd tried two other inns already. The road to the Forbidden Fortress was teeming with travelers. Degarius couldn't bear the thought of trying to sleep in the cramped coach. One room was enough. He'd sleep on the floor.

"I can squeeze your coachman in the bunkroom. Dinner," the innkeeper wagged his head apologetically as he took Miss Nazar's coat, "is mutton stew and dilled potatoes. It's all the soldiers have left me. And no wine. Well..." He glanced to Miss Nazar, to the jewels around her neck. "Let me see what I can do." He flagged the serving girl. "Show them to a table."

The serving girl sat them at the end of a long, empty table and then returned with the stew and dilled potatoes. The innkeeper followed with two small pewter cups. He winked as he sat them down and motioned for her to try it.

The drink looked like strong tea, but from the potent smell, Degarius guessed it Gherian corn liquor. Miss Nazar took a sip. Her face bloomed with simple warmth, but not with giddiness. The night before a big battle, many men were merry, as if they were sticking their tongues out at fate. She wasn't like that. She was like the quiet men who made a knot of fear, pulling the threads tighter and tighter, hoping they wouldn't come undone. The danger was they'd pull too hard and snap the strings. She'd said she wasn't afraid of death, that she'd seen it many times. Lerouge and Kieran had died in front of her. But she sure as hell was afraid of failing. She had a tender conscience. How had he ever doubted her when she said she'd never loved Lerouge? Even if she had loved the prince, it shouldn't have mattered to him. She ultimately denied Lerouge whatever affections he might have gained, denied herself a position of amazing wealth and power, and stayed bound to Solace. What inconceivable trial had loving him, Nan, been to her that she had to forsake her profession because of it? Well, she was a Maker-be-damned fool for imagining him a good man worth whatever tears her conscience had shed.

Her thanks to the innkeeper, given in Gherian, recalled Degarius. At her gentle smile, the innkeeper's fleshy neck turned redder at the collar. "The drinks weren't for my benefit," he said as soon as the innkeeper left.

"You'll like it."

Degarius tilted his cup. The liquid left a thin, glossy film behind. Its heat was just spreading down his throat when four swaggering bluecoats came in—a captain and his three lieutenants. By their exaggerated gestures and loud voices, they'd succeeded in finding drinks, ample drinks, somewhere. There was no place for them other than at their table. Damn. He thought about getting up and leaving, but that'd bring more questions than it avoided. Sure enough, the serving girl was bringing them their way. Degarius glanced to their insignias. None of them was in regiments he'd met. Good. He stood to acknowledge them. They all bowed to Miss Nazar before sitting.

The captain, who had one sunken, closed eye, came beside Degarius and asked, "Cabinetman?"

"Yes," Degarius said and tried to disguise his dismay at being mistaken twice in one day for one of the soft-armed, paunchy-stomached breed of men who served as bureaucrats. He nodded to Miss Nazar. "She wants to attend the Solemnity."

The Gherian leaned to Degarius. His breath, reeking to Zadora of beer, was hot in Degarius's ear. "Ah, the Solemnity. Our Alenius has a big surprise planned for sunset. I can't wait until the Sarapostans see it."

The taste of the liquor went sour in Degarius's mouth. "What kind of big surprise?"

The captain seemed not to hear, and Degarius understood why. His beer-glazed single eye was narrowed on Miss Nazar, and he was stroking his straw-colored mustache. The bastard was undressing Ari with his eye. Degarius made a fist under the table, but forced himself to be calm. The captain might have information. "I've heard rumors about this surprise. It's in the Forbidden Fortress?"

The Gherian puffed his chest. "I've been to the Forbidden Fortress. Received my captaincy from the sovereign himself. I've seen what's in his private garden. Didn't get into the atrium. He has that shut up tighter..." The serving girl put a dish of stew before the Gherian. He speared a piece of mutton, and as if he'd completely forgotten his previous train of thought, said, "A fellow like you could get a good commission, have his own regiment. But I suppose not everyone hears the call to duty. You cabinetmen must tend to your own riches."

"One of my ears is half-deaf, but I hear the call of duty." Degarius raised his glasses off his nose. "Alenius, however, doesn't want blind men leading his troops."

The captain laughed. "I had but one eye when I was made captain. You've got two and aren't blind enough to take an ugly wife." He was looking at Miss Nazar again with an unmistakable glint in his eye—and she'd seen it. Her cheeks flamed, and she was looking at her plate to avoid the Gherian captain's scrutiny. The captain rapped once on the table to get her attention and asked, "Do you play cards?"

She put her fork down. "I don't speak much Gherian."

"Why doesn't she speak Gherian?" he asked Degarius. "Is she a southerner?"

Degarius nodded. "I'm from the borderlands."

"Then you better watch your wife. Heathens are heathens, you know. Does she cheat at cards?" The Gherian reached into his coat, pulled out a deck of cards, and arched his brows at Arvana. Because of his missing eye, the action looked particularly grotesque.

Degarius bristled, but said coolly, "My *wife* doesn't play cards." The old, stout innkeeper's admiration was one thing. To him she was a rich guest. He'd charge them a small fortune for the drinks. This captain's was another, and Degarius had had enough of it. He downed the last of the liquor, stood and said, "If you'll pardon us."

Without hesitation, Miss Nazar rose from the table. How beautiful she was. The noble way she held her chin seemed meant to tell the Gherian that he was a sorry second to the man she was with. He laced his arm around her waist and raised his free hand to the soldiers. "Good luck on the campaign."

"Leave your wife upstairs and play a round of Waero," the captain called to cover his defeat.

As she walked, her hip swayed under Degarius's firmly placed hand. Feeling in sudden generous humor, he called back, "Only when I have coin to lose."

When out of the dining room, Miss Nazar said, "I'm sorry you didn't get to finish your dinner. Thank you. I'm not used to that kind of...men never..." She touched the low-cut neck of the gown and Degarius's gaze went there. A bewildering mix of understanding and desire made his head swim, but then she twisted free of his hand. "You don't have to pretend anymore. They can't see us."

❈❈❈

Arvana waited behind Degarius as he unlocked the room. The ribbon on his ponytail was coming untied. His broad shoulders hunched so he could get nearer the keyhole. Why couldn't he have said one kind word when she told him he didn't have to pretend anymore? She had given him the chance. But he'd said nothing, just asked the innkeeper for the room key. What had she expected?

The door opened and she followed him in. The room was clean but small and sparsely furnished with a bed, washstand, and a bench before the lit fireplace, which Degarius went straight away to stoke. Their trunk, sitting under the window, had been delivered. Arvana uncrossed her arms. It was austere, but cozy. Maybe she could sleep tonight, on the eve of going to the Forbidden Fortress. It felt like the one safe place in Gheria, safe from the leering soldier, the impending war, the draeden and The Scyon.

"I'll sleep on the floor," Degarius said.

She didn't argue, though after the moons of sleeping on the ground it wouldn't have bothered her to take the floor. "Do you need anything out of the trunk?" she asked as she opened it.

"My toothbrush."

She searched through Mrs. Karlkin's packing and the leather riding breeches they'd brought just in case they'd be taking the horses back from the Forbidden Fortress. She found his nightshirt, the toothbrushes, and a nightgown, yet another of Lina's old things, yellowed and trimmed with fussy, itchy-feeling lace. "Do you want your nightshirt?"

"I'll sleep in these," he said of the breeches he was wearing. "I have another pair, right?"

"Yes." The simple word *yes* felt odd as she spoke it. They were speaking about the mundane things of a life spent together. She unfolded her nightgown and held the shoulders to hers. "Do you mind?"

"Oh. While you change, I'll get water." He took the pitcher and left the room.

Arvana tossed the nightgown on the bed and reached to the back of her neck to remove the necklace. Ugh. She pried at the clasp every different way, but it didn't release. If she pulled any harder, it might break. Why had he burdened her with this thing? He was going to have to take it off. If he broke it, it wouldn't be her fault.

Wrenching her elbow behind her back, she started to unbutton the dress. She managed the bottom buttons and the top three, but no matter how she strained her shoulders, she couldn't reach the ones in the middle. When Mrs. Karlkin had helped her into it, she hadn't thought of the trouble it'd be to take off. What a stupid way to fashion a garment. She hated Lina's dresses. Hated that they seemed to give the Gheria permission to leer at her. Hated that she couldn't take them off herself. She sank on the bench in front of the fire.

Degarius knocked on the door before entering. Well, he wasn't going to catch her in any state of undress. Not with three stubborn buttons in the middle of her back. She rose and crossed her arms. "I can't get off this ridiculous dress. Or the necklace. The clasp is stuck."

He sat the pitcher down and said, "Turn around."

She pulled her hair to one side so he could see the necklace's clasp.

"I need more light. Turn sideways to the fire," he said.

The clasp clicked open. His fingers and the necklace lifted away from her skin. His arms reached around her and he held the necklace in front of her to take. It had been a weight around her neck and heart all day. Her stomach went hollow at having to accept it again, and this time from his hands. "Your father said it was your mother's," she blurted. "I don't want to be responsible for it. It must mean a great deal to you. You brought it as a keepsake, but I can't bear the thought that if something happens to it, it's my fault."

"What are you talking about?"

She couldn't face him. "You brought it as a keepsake of something good in your life, of your mother. I don't know. A reminder that there are things worth fighting for."

He laughed uneasily. "Don't you know what a gift is?"

Not this argument again. "Most people don't give gifts via their housekeeper who's told to say 'Here, you need this to look proper.'"

He said nothing.

"I don't want to be the caretaker of anything else." Why was every burden thrust on her? His medal. The Blue Eye. Her father in his last, unbearable days. His mother's engagement jewels. She wanted to throw the damn necklace against the wall. Who cared how expensive it was or what it meant to him? It was nothing to her. She spun around and grasping the necklace in her fist, struck it to his chest. "Take it back." His hand flew to hers. She wanted to pull away, fling the necklace to the floor, but he pressed her fist harder into his chest. "I don't want it."

"All of this is my family's fault. I wanted to make it up to you somehow."

"I never blamed *you*," she said and darted a spiteful look to him, but he wore a look she'd never seen on his face before. The penitence in his eyes took her breath and anger away.

"I had to do this the only way I could," he said.

"I never blamed you."

"I know. It is a gift. Please keep it."

"I can't."

"You're not a Solacian anymore."

She dropped her chin to her chest and closed her eyes. She wasn't a Solacian anymore. "I don't know what I am."

"Ari." His fingertips lighted on her brow and traced down over her temple.

She opened her eyes. His face was so close. Though he'd said he gave the necklace and ring to her in compensation for her having to deal with the aftermath of Lina's choices, his touch and his eyes said otherwise. His thumb grazed across her bottom lip, a whisper of a touch, but her heart raced. Her eyelids drifted shut, and she leaned forward to meet his mouth, and after one tentative brush of their lips, it was as if a rainstorm opened up inside her. She couldn't be tender. A downpour couldn't be a shower. She kissed him hard, tasted the liquor that was still on his tongue.

He pushed her hand still holding the necklace from his chest and drew her body full into his. His hands swept inside the unbuttoned top of the back of her dress, almost tearing at the thin fabric of her chemise. He kissed into the deep recess between her jaw and neck while his hands moved down her body to her hips.

Then, in a motion of pure grace, he dropped to his knees before her. He took the necklace from her hand, put it on the bench, and gazed up at her with a look that made her ache with emptiness. She reached to the bodice of the dress and pulled out the relic and took if off. That wasn't her burden now, either.

She lifted his glasses from his face. Would his eyes never cease to startle her? She bent to put the glasses and relic on the bed.

His arms encircled her waist and his forearms reached up her back. Gathering her to him, he buried his face in her body. His chest heaved with hard breaths against her.

Arvana pulled the already loose binding from his ponytail and ran her fingers through his hair, warm and soft next to his scalp, deliciously cool at the ends. How wonderful his face felt, the day-grown stubble rough in one direction, smooth in the other. She ran her forefinger over the ridges of his bottom teeth. Everything, she wanted to know everything about him.

Like the wind takes a leaf and floats it to the ground, she felt as if something outside of her own force eased her to her knees. Her hands were on his shoulders, so wide and powerful. After slipping her fingers under his jacket, she kneaded the thick muscles at the sides of his neck until his head lolled back and he exhaled a long sigh. She took the jacket's lapels, opened them wide, and eased them over his shoulders. He shook his arms from the sleeves and sloughed the jacket behind him. She pulled the ribbon closing the collar of his blouse, and, looking into his eyes, gave a silent command he obeyed in one swift motion—he untucked his blouse from his trousers and billowed it over his head. He wasn't embarrassed or self-conscious. Why should he be? He'd worked long and endured much to be strong. The firelight glowed on the swells of his muscles. Arms hanging to his sides, he became still, allowed her eyes to linger on the scar across his chest, then her finger to trace its length. His body was a book of stories, but it wasn't time to hear them now.

Degarius took her hand from where it rested on his chest over his heart and kissed her fingers, one by one. Did she know how beautiful she was and what it did to him? Though he'd dreamed of this night after night, his imagination was a damned inferior thing. It never really knew the intoxicating smell of her. How indescribably soft her skin was. The sensation ignited by her finger skimming down his chest. He reached around and undid the buttons she hadn't been able to reach. Her back arched at his touch. He edged the dress from one of her shoulders. Her hand didn't rush to return it to place. Instead, she flexed her shoulders together and allowed him to pull one sleeve, then the next from her arms. The dress fell in a pool about her knees.

He spread his jacket behind her, wadded his shirt into a pillow, then laid a hand to her shoulder and guided her backward until she lay on the floor atop the bed he'd made. Her hair fanned in glorious dark auburn waves over the white of his shirt. She titled up her hips and he eased the dress from her. The filmy, white chemise she wore underneath the dress reached midthigh. Her back arched when he lightly stroked from her knee to her breast. There was a Maker and a paradise, but they sure as hell didn't have anything to do with being dead. Then, as he'd thought of doing a thousand times, he knelt straddling her thighs and started to push the chemise up when she held up a hand, palm out, as if she was going to say no. But she laid her hand on his stomach and traced down the fine line of hair to his breeches.

"I want to know," she said.

"I do, too," he replied and kissed her.

SNOW

Degarius woke to warmth, to the softness of her body curled into his, and went hard with desire. He wanted to love her again and again. Would there be any greater sweetness than to wake to this every morning of his life? He eased to his elbow. In the faint morning light, her hair was a dark tangle upon the pillow. Should he wake her? He reached to brush her hair from her neck to kiss it but then saw the chain around her neck and remembered where he was and why. She hadn't forgotten. She'd been up during the night and put on the damned thing.

What the hell kind of man was he, taking her to the Forbidden Fortress to battle not just a draeden, but The Scyon? After his battle with the immature poison draeden, by some miracle, an old healer at the Outpost had saved his feet. He had nearly lost them, and when he first had to stand upon them, the pain was so excruciating that he almost wished he had. What would the fire draeden do to her? It was unbearable to imagine. What if she carried the beginning of their child? She wasn't with moon blood, so it was possible.

He rolled to his back and the heat of her body dissipated from his. Why the hell couldn't they just leave this mission to someone else? Hundreds of thousands depended upon them, but why and how had they become their responsibility? Why must they sacrifice their own happiness for others they didn't love, or even know? Because fate had put the damn relics in their hands before they met. Perhaps if they just walked away from *this*, they would be happy together for a time, but blackness would eat their consciences and love once the draeden set upon the world. Damn it, why was he even thinking about this. What did she say last night? She wanted to know, know *before*...damn the Maker. She had never lain with a man. When she woke, would she regret it? Of course, she would. She was good. Though she gave up her novice's ring, she never broke her vows until last night. She couldn't even accept the necklace. How could she accept making love to a man who hadn't promised to be her husband, had used her only for his pleasure? *Damn it, that's not true.* Still, he hoped she regretted it, hoped she despised him, because he couldn't bear a look of tenderness when he had to hand her into the coach this morning for the last time.

He eased out of bed. It was freezing. He found his breeches, pulled them on, then dropped to the floor to do his morning push-ups, but his coat was there and the memory of her lying upon it. He put on his blouse and the coat and then gathered her dress and chemise. Before laying them on the foot of the bed, he held them to his face to smell her body one more time. Then, as quietly as he could, he made a fire.

What time was it? He went to the window and widened the narrow slit in the drapery. It was snowing. Damn it all to hell. Snow. "We need to get going."

❊ ❊ ❊

The voice floated into Arvana's half-awake mind. She thought she'd not slept at all, but here she was opening her eyes. The covers were thrown back from Nan's side of the bed. Watery-gray morning light lit the room. As she rolled over, a cold spot in the sheets glided over her breasts, a sudden reminder that she was naked except for the Blue Eye. After Nan fell asleep, she'd gingerly moved his heavy arm from her chest and crept around the bed to retrieve the relic. If a thief stole in, she'd never forgive herself for what some would already say the Maker held as an unforgivable act.

Dressed, Nan was looking out the window. He'd made a fire and laid her clothes over the foot of the bed. He must have been awake for some time, perhaps already finishing the countless push-ups she'd seen him do every morning in Cumberland.

He hadn't stayed in bed with her.

"It's snowing," he said without turning to her.

Snow? She hadn't seen snow since leaving Sylvania. "Is there much on the ground?"

"Not yet, but I'd like to leave as soon as we can."

Sitting up, Arvana held the blanket to her chest. It seemed ridiculous asking him to leave the room while she dressed, considering what happened last night. Still, she'd feel foolish climbing out of bed, naked and shivering. He was standing there, hands clasped behind his back, as if nothing had happened—or, as if everything had happened and staring out the window was all he could do. She couldn't tell.

She grabbed the chemise, pulled it over her head, and unfurled it to her waist. She shimmied it over her hips. There, she could get up. She peeled the covers back and swept her feet to the floor. Brown dry blood streaked the inside of her thighs and bottom sheet. After the fire had dimmed, he'd lifted her to the bed and loved her again beneath the warm covers. She had ruined the sheets and her body was dirty. The ugliness of both stains embarrassed her. The lining of his coat, too, must be stained. It wasn't moon blood; it wasn't that time. It was the part of her body she'd once sworn to keep intact as a sign she'd not be distracted by lust from the purer love of the Maker. She smoothed the chemise down and yanked the covers over the bed stains.

Facing away from him, she stepped into the dress. As soon as she'd arranged the skirt, she heard him walking toward her. He'd been listening, waiting for her dress to be ready for buttoning. His fingers touched the bottom button, and she began to tremble. What if he wanted to love her again? He would see the stains. She held her body rigid, but she had to fight to keep her breathing calm. Any moment, he'd kiss her neck. He wouldn't mind the stains. They were from his body, too. Her spine tingled in mixed dread and expectation.

His fingers just went from button to button. Perhaps when he reached the top he'd linger on her skin. But his fingers lifted, and she heard him step away. The tingling changed to a chill.

"One more thing." She bent, picked up the necklace, and held it to him. A small hope glimmered that he'd close the clasp, and his arms, around her.

Without ceremony, he fastened it and walked away.

She crossed her arms tight across her chest. She'd been wrong at not taking him for his word that he gave her the jewels to atone for the burden Lina's past put on her. Without turning to look at him, she said, "I need to wash. It won't take long."

"I'm going to order the coach. I'll see if there's any coffee," he said and left.

From the trunk, she removed her toothbrush and the breeches and boots she was to wear under her dress—in case they needed to ride from the Forbidden Fortress on horseback. She sat the breeches on the bed.

At the washstand, she brushed her teeth. A cloth wetted, she lifted her skirt and dabbed at the stains from his body and hers. How had she come to this? To standing alone in a cold room in Gheria, wiping away remnants of a forbidden deed? How could she have felt so full and complete last night, but empty and alone this morning? Everything she'd learned in Solace had warned her against the destructive, soul-gnawing power of lust. She'd recalled the lesson just moments ago, but promptly forgot it again at his touch. She didn't blame Degarius. She'd said she wanted to know what it was to be with a man, and he'd obliged, twice. There *was* truth in it, but who was she fooling? She did want to know, but not about what it would be like to lay with *any* man. Just him. Once, she had wanted so fervently to be a shacra, and now she was scrubbing the last bit of brown from her legs. Visions of Hell hadn't stopped her. There, her thighs were clean, but were a raw red from rubbing. She folded the stains to the inside of the washcloth, laid it over the bowl's rim, and took the comb she'd set out. Though the washstand had a small mirror, out of habit, she combed her hair without looking until the teeth caught in a snarl of tangled ends. As she leaned to the mirror to pick apart the knot of hair, she recalled how proud she'd been of her hair, how she thought Payter admired her for it. She'd gone on the sleigh without a hat just so the beauty of her hair would snare him. The teeth of the comb caught and snapped several hairs, but the tangle remained. By the Maker, it was a stubborn knot. She'd gone on the sleigh ride without a hat to show off her beauty. It had been nothing but trouble and vanity, this hair. It was what the superior should have taken from her. But she'd have looked like a prostitute with her hair shorn. They cropped their hair as a sign of cleanliness, not of sin. She wasn't clean. The washcloth and bed sheets were stained. But if she cut her hair, severed the knot, she would be clean, free from the vanity that feeds lust.

The trunk still open, she found his shaving kit and took the razor. The blade was folded into ivory scales. Like everything he owned, it was simple but lovely and of high quality. Yet, he wasn't owned by his things. He hardly seemed to note them. He was more a monk than she ever was a Solacian. His duty came before everything, even the home to which he did seem attached. She recalled the beauty of Ferne Clyffe, the pleasing way he'd situated the barns and the pretty bridge he'd had built after Lina passed. It was no sin to build a place that elevated one's spirit here on this earth. What else was Solace? At the remembrance of the place, and how the draeden burned it, the reason why she was in the Gherian inn wormed its way back to the fore of her mind. She had to be quick about what she wanted to do; he would be waiting to leave for the Forbidden Fortress. After unfolding the razor blade from its ivory scales, she parted out a section of hair, held it out from her skull, and brought the razor to it. Finally, she'd have forsaken everything. Though she wore a fine dress and jewels, they didn't belong to her and she didn't desire them. Certainly, she didn't desire the Blue Eye. She touched the band of his ring. No, she didn't want that, either. Then, it struck her it was the only thing she hadn't removed last night. Grief swelled behind her eyes, making her head feel ten times heavier than she'd imagined it was by being burdened with hair. She placed her thumb upon the top of the blade to refold it when the door opened behind her.

Rapid footsteps approached.

She lowered the still-open razor to the table as she fluttered between the joy of him returning and embarrassment about the razor. What was she to say on either account? *Oh Ari, what does it matter.* He was back. She turned around.

The one-eyed Gherian captain was a blur of motion before her. He pressed his hand over her mouth, then pushed her into the table and bent her spine.

She felt for the razor, grasped it, and brought it to the small of her back.

"Don't yell," he whispered in Gherian, his breath bitter with coffee.

As she nodded, she brought the razor around, aiming to get in at his neck from beneath where he'd raised his arm to hold her mouth shut.

He lowered his elbow, knocking the razor off course. With his free hand, he grabbed hers and squeezing hard, wrenched her wrist to point the blade's edge toward her face. She had to stop fighting. If her strength failed, the blade would gouge her. He guided it almost effortlessly to her eye. The blade was so close it was a blur. "Scream and I cut your tongue out. I have cut out the tongues of fifty men. I know how to do it."

The socket of his missing eye puckered as he narrowed his good eye at her. "I hate cabinetmen and heathens. A heathen girl took my eye. A fine Gherian blue eye." He kept talking, but the words began to come too fast for her to understand.

To gain a space from the blade, she arched back even more over the table. He moved the blade from between her eyes, to her lips, then back to her eyes. His single eye danced its gaze between her eyes and lips. His mouth twisted with wicked indecision. He was trying to decide whether to put out her eyes or cut out her tongue first.

There was no second-guessing on her part—she had to use the relic. She moved her free left hand slowly from the table where she'd been using it to brace herself, to her side, then to her stomach.

He sucked air loudly into his nose. "You smell good. You're afraid. I like that. I'm going to put out both your eyes. But this one first."

As he shifted the blade to her right eye, she found the relic and for once was glad that the dress was cut so low.

She pressed the latch.

CHOSEN

The Forbidden Fortress, Gheria

In his private room, Master Nils sat at his desk and swallowed a spoon of gruel. It stuck in his throat. Everything stuck in his throat, even gruel. He forced a cough and spit half of what he'd just eaten into a napkin. Worse yet, his nose began to fill with the gruel. He wadded the spit into a corner of the napkin, then used a clean part to blow his nose. It was humiliating doing this in front of even someone so lowly as the asher. Why had he come at this inopportune time? "Is it important?" His voice gurgled as he spoke.

"Yes, My Excellency," the asher said.

"My nose runs when I eat." Nils coughed again and picked through the napkin for an unused spot. "Shut the door." His voice was clearer. "Now, tell me has happened?"

The asher closed the door. "Just after sunrise a Lily Girl was sent to fetch Rorke to the sovereign's bedchamber. The sovereign was beside himself, shouting that the woman with the Blue Eye wasn't dead. He'd seen her with a man he recognized. Juvenot was his name. I gather he is a soldier because the sovereign sent for Aleniusson to learn where this Juvenot was stationed. Then he told Rorke that if he could find this woman, the Blue Eye would be his, just as promised."

So, the Blue Eye was in Gheria and likely coming straight to Rorke's hands, if he could get his hands upon it. He'd have every spy in the kingdom looking for this woman. Well, not every spy. Nils still had his own little contingent and the asher was one of his most recent recruits. Hearing of Rorke's abuse of the boy, he'd had the storeroom steward request him for an apprentice, but once he was within the sovereign's compound, he'd had his duty changed to being an escort for the Lily Girls in the secret tunnels. The asher was quite good at listening outside the tunnel doors. "You've done a fine job..." He searched his memory for the boy's name, but he could only ever remember him as an asher.

"There are strange, bad things in this place," said the boy. "Is the Blue Eye the sovereign spoke of what the Judges used to steal souls during the Reckoning?"

"So it seems, asher. So it seems. This place isn't what it used to be. I was the sovereign's man in waiting before I became the first cleric. I was the one who gave Alenius kindness and good counsel when all others around him were false, even his own mother, even his love, that hateful girl Breena. His mother despised Breena, in part because she was a commoner, but mostly because the girl had a thirst for nobility and power. Alenius was nothing more than her foolish pawn. When his mother found out she was with child, they had a great fight and the girl accidently backed into a candlestick."

"What happened to her?"

"She was badly burned and died a slow, terrible death. Against my advice, he tried to bring her back with the Beckoner. I myself put it in her decayed chest. But it was too late. Too late. And now, after all I've done, Rorke is his pet. I was the one people courted. They came to me for favors because I was the gatekeeper to the sovereign. You should have seen the payments I required. Mountains of gold and jewels. Fine furs. But I gave them all up to take care of the Fortress clerics. Now it is Rorke who has the sovereign's ear and the gifts are showered on him, but he keeps it all and lives like a heathen king."

"Rorke is a bad man."

"And you are a good boy for telling me what Rorke does. The Eternal Master is pleased with the truth." Nils thought he should give the boy a reward. Any small thing would make the asher grateful. A ceremonial knife might be just the thing. It commemorated many men's sacrifices. Nils, his sight not what it used to be, had stopped performing the cutting several years back after he'd botched one boy. Now, it was just another reminder of what he couldn't do. He opened his desk drawer and shuffled through the papers for a white box. Where was it? Had someone taken it? He reached far to the back, but it wasn't there, either. He started again through the papers. Ah, there at the side. He pushed aside the gruel and napkin and placed the long, slender box upon the desk. "Open it."

The asher opened the box and removed a small, curved blade knife with a mother of pearl handle in a white leather sheath. He drew the knife from the cover and said, "The blade is rusted."

"Draw it through an onion a few times."

The boy nodded, resheathed the knife, and returned it to the box.

"You know what kind of knife it is?"

"I remember that kind of knife very well. I was only made this spring. Thank you, My Excellency."

"Tell me, is today the last day of the Winter Solemnity?"

"It is."

Then it was time to act. Everything was starting over—the calendar, the very order of the world. And he would have a place in this new order.

Because he was old, he'd been pushed aside. Aleniusson had received Paulus's sword, Assaea. And now Rorke was on the verge of having a Blue Eye. The sovereign had awarded them these gifts to satisfy their need for power and to keep them enemies with each other, and not him. But they were fools to think the sovereign would let them keep the relics for long. The sovereign didn't think his oldest and most loyal servant was still a capable player in this game, so he'd been given nothing, though the sovereign owed all his knowledge of the ancient arts to him. Nils had been the one to find the texts, to learn the secrets of the Beckoner and the creation of the draeden. And he'd not forgotten one word of it. Nils guessed he had at least another few years left in him—long enough to see to the maturation of a new draeden. "Go and make your morning prayers," he said to the asher, "but stay close. Later you'll be needed to escort a Lily to the sovereign's bedchamber."

"But I haven't made my absolution yet."

"You will want to wait."

Six Lily Girls stood in a line before Nils. All were tall, blonde, and youthfully lithe as had been Alenius's long dead love, Breena. At one time, Nils would have been picky about which girl he chose, looking for the one who not only most physically resembled Breena, but the one whose character was most like hers: outspoken and domineering. Now, he hadn't taken time to know them like he used to and they all had a sameness of appearance. It didn't matter, though. Alenius had made a man of himself with the Beckoner, a man with an easily stimulated appetite.

Out of habit, Nils made a show of smelling the girls, touching their skin and hair, looking at their teeth. The aged Lilies, their instructors, sat in a semicircle of chairs. Each hoped her protégé would be chosen, as it earned her new finery and an extra draught of burned wine for two moons. He turned to these instructors. "Which is most ripe?"

They knew to tell the truth lest he checked by daubing a handkerchief between the girl's legs, checking for the telltale clear wetness.

One of the old Lilies, Mathilde, pointed. "On the end. You will find her to your satisfaction."

Nils went to the last girl. Her jaw trembled when his finger pushed her lower lip down so he might see her bottom teeth. Ah, might not a bit of fear be a good thing? Make her more susceptible to threat? "Today the sovereign will request you. Bathe, perfume yourself with rabian oil, bead your hair with a hundred sapphires, and make your face as white as snow and your lips as deep red as sweet cherries."

She curtsied and replied something in such a thin voice that Nils couldn't hear her.

"Rejoice that you are the chosen one on the day of the sovereign's triumph," he said as a reply that would be appropriate no matter what the girl had muttered.

The dismissed line filed to their rooms.

Nils turned to the aged Lilies. "Mathilde, stay and chat with me." Unlike many other old Lilies, she hadn't grown indolent, or any less ruthless, with time. Good. When the rest were gone, he grasped her outstretched hands. "Dear friend." Rings covered her cold, bony fingers. Determined to keep her youthful figure, she had many years ago already aged into more skeleton than woman. "How would you like to spend the rest of your days among the world on your own estate?"

She pulled from his hands. "What is the price for such freedom? I've heard it was offered in the past but at great expense." She referenced Lina. Though the official story was that Lina had taken ill and died, word from the outside world always eventually filtered back into the compound via new Lilies and indiscreet clerics.

"There is no expense to you, unless you fail at what I ask."

"And what is that, dear Nils?" she said with a mix of charm and suspicion.

"You order your student to do two things. When the sovereign beds her, she must imagine the person she hates most in this world. Most likely, it will be me. She will give in to fear, to disgust, and imagine the most horrible disease consuming this person. She must picture him growing ill quickly, with blood seeping from his every orifice. Afterward, to ensure the seed takes root, she must remain in the sovereign's bed until I fetch her. If her next moon blood fails to flow, I will immediately grant her the same freedom I promised you and special protection for the babe she carries."

"The sovereign means to birth a wasting draeden?"

"So it seems."

"Will my Lily not die from the disease it carries?"

"The mother is immune. She will never have to worry."

"And what if she refuses or doesn't become pregnant?"

"My clerics will kill her family. And you, you will always fear every sip of burned wine."

Mathilde sighed. "What time must she be ready?"

"She is my gift to him in celebration of the ending of the Winter Solemnity. Bring her to the bedchamber this evening as he dresses for the meeting with the cabinetmen." What a gift she would be, one to himself, one that bestowed on Alenius an apt reward for his disloyalty. For all history, the despised wasting draeden would tarnish Alenius's claim as a benevolent god. "Don't forget." Nils tapped his temple. "I forget many things these days. But I won't forget this."

※-※-※

The Inn in Gheria

The coach driver's voice came through the door. "Lord Degarius sent me up for the trunk."

"A moment. I'm not ready," Arvana called. Her voice had sounded tremulous. Would he notice?

What was she to do with the body? If it was discovered, they'd be detained and asked a thousand questions. Shove him beneath the bed. It was where the monsters of childhood lived, amidst the dust and dark.

She got upon her knees and first pushed him by the shoulder and then by the thigh. Though he was thin, he was still a dead weight and a strain to move. His feet caught upon the footboard. No matter how she tried, she couldn't get the knees to bend so that the feet could be hidden. The driver was waiting. There was nothing to do but cover the rest of the Gherian as best she could. She pulled the bedclothes half off the bed, leaving the stain still covered, and arranged them to hide the underside and protruding feet.

Leery of the bed, she sat upon the floor to put on the leather riding breeches and boots. She collected her toothbrush and comb and flung them into the trunk. The razor lay on the floor where it fell from the stricken Gherian's hand. She kicked it into the fireplace, then answered the door.

"You look a bit put out, miss."

Arvana put on her fur hat. "I overslept and rushed."

The answer seemed to satisfy him. She put on her coat and waited as he grappled the trunk out the door so she could close it. Please, let the maid take her time in coming to tidy the room.

As she came downstairs, the aromas of coffee and fresh bread drifted up to meet her. Usually, she was starving in the morning, but today her stomach felt like a small, hard stone. Would the Gherian captain's friends be waiting? Did they know of his plan?

The soldiers from last night were there. She held her breath as she walked past, trying to read their faces and not seem that she noticed them.

Several looked at her, but it seemed more of a casual taking notice of a woman than a wondering of what had happened between her and their Gherian captain. She felt shameful just thinking of it, as if it had somehow been her fault.

Past them, she exhaled. Degarius, absently nursing a cup, was across the room sitting by a window, his eye to the weather like the other guests. How was she ever to tell him that she'd had to use the Blue Eye?

✦ ✦ ✦

Degarius sat down his coffee cup. She stood at the edge of the table, her face pale. She glanced to the door, couldn't even bring herself to look at him, let alone sit with him to eat the bread and coffee he ordered for her. It was as he told himself it would be. She despised him, and likely herself, for last night. The coffee went rancid in his mouth.

WEIGHTLESS

Gheria

A rvana rubbed her glove against the fogged-over coach window and peered out the clear circle but couldn't see Degarius. All day he'd been taking turns with the driver guiding the team through the snow. The journey that should have been a matter of hours had turned into an all-day ordeal. They had to get to the Fortress before sundown when the Gherian day ended and the New Year began, when Alenius made his announcement. And she still had to tell him about the Blue Eye. It wasn't just the dread about potentially losing all of their advantage of surprise; it seemed impossible to speak of the Gherian, of what he intended.

The coach slid sideways. She braced her back against the seat. The stomach-churning motion stopped. They were lumbering forward again. She hated being inside, at the mercy of the driver.

Supposedly, he was a good coachman, had driven a
hay wagon through drifts up to his waist. Just as she
was reassuring herself the coach made a hard
bump. It violently heaved to a stop, flinging her to
the floor.

The door flew open and in whipped a blast of
cold air and snow.

"Are you all right?" Degarius asked

"What happened?" Arvana uncrumpled.

"There's a big rut in the road. The front wheels
are caught."

She edged to the door.

"What are you doing?" he asked.

"Getting out to make the coach lighter."

Snow caked Degarius's hat and hair and his
cheeks burned bright red. How cold his feet must
be.

The coach ahead of them disappeared into the
curtain of snow. Was another behind in this
forsaken weather to help them if they couldn't get
free? To one side was a thick stand of trees, to the
other, an endless field. No one was near to help
them. If they couldn't free themselves by sunset,
they'd not only miss getting to the Fortress on
time, but also probably freeze to death. What a
cruel twist of fate it would be if they perished on
the road, almost to the Forbidden Fortress. Not
defeated by The Scyon or a draeden but the
weather.

The eerie sound of slowly splintering wood crackled through air. The scent of pine wafted thick. Wet and heavy snow was snapping the pines.

"If we weren't in this ridiculous coach, we'd have made it through the rut like everyone else." Degarius circled the coach to examine the wheels and crouched to look at the axle. "Everything's fine. On my mark, pull her out a bit." He shouldered under the coach. With a grunt, he tried to stand straight. "Now."

The wheels spun against the snow-packed edge of the rut. Degarius strained harder. His face and neck were crimson and his grimace was painful to see. The wheels raised a fraction but nowhere near enough.

The driver yelled, "Whoa."

Arvana trudged to the driver. She didn't have to be a useless woman, standing and watching. That had never been her lot. "I'm going to drive. You help Lord Degarius."

The coachman stared.

"Don't worry. I won't run over you."

Still red-faced and heaving frosty breaths, Degarius motioned for the coachman to join him.

Arvana climbed to the seat. It'd been forever since she'd had a team in hand, but she knew the commands intuitively. She hoped the Sarapostans had the good sense to train their horses the proper way. She glanced backward. The men were digging the snow away from the wheels. She took the reins and titled her head back. The snow seemed to come from one point directly above, not very high up. Flakes landed on her cheeks and lips, released their bursts of cold, and then melted. She used to think snow was beautiful, the Maker's breath.

That all changed twelve years ago.

Her feet stung with cold and her hands numbly grasped the shovel; freezing wetness had long ago soaked through her gloves. But she'd cleared the snow down to the crunchy brown stalks of dead grass. She planted the point of the shovel in the ground and with one boot on its top edge, put her weight into breaking the frozen soil.

The shovel dug in a finger's width.

With both feet, she jumped onto the shovel.

The ground wouldn't give. It had to!

Her breath a heavy mist, she thrust the shovel repeatedly, trying to chisel into the unyielding earth, but it kept hitting the dirt with a dull *thud*.

She flung the shovel away, dropped to her knees, and clawed at the bits of loose snow and dirt. The gloves were too thick, so she pulled them off. Her hands were raw from the friction of shoveling with wet gloves, so she dug with her nails that she had kept so lovely smooth to play the kithara. She dug and dug, but the hole wasn't even big enough to bury a coffee cup.

What was she to do? Her father had been dead three days. She teetered sideways and fell on her side into the bank of snow she had shoveled from the plot.

Cold through and through, she turned her face to the sky. It was the purest, unending blue. Dear Maker, was there not a place for her there? It was so vast, clean and peaceful, and she was so dreadfully tired of the tiny house and the unspeakable smells and sights within. Surely she had suffered enough, chipped away the soiled parts of her spirit, so that it was so light that the Maker would lift her into that beautiful oblivion where her father must be. The rigid corpse in the house wasn't he. But no one lifted her. She just grew colder and a realization crept into her with the cold. She hadn't done enough yet to get rid of the guilt of going on the sleigh ride. And her care of her father hadn't been pure. She wished him to die because of his misery, but also her own.

❈－❈－❈

"Get your shoulder up under the chassis," Degarius called to the driver.

Arvana blinked the snow from her eyelashes. She peered over the side of the coach. The driver had taken his place.

Degarius began, "One, two...higher...higher. Now."

With a gentle shake of the reins, she started the horses forward and the coach moved. The men leaped out of the way. The bigger back wheels dipped into the rut but cleared it. They were free.

The driver, doing a high-stepping jog through the deep snow, and a slogging Degarius came alongside.

She engaged the brake and halted the horses.

The driver nodded his thanks. "Cheer up, miss. Not much farther. I'll have you safe and warm in no time. Need a hand down?"

The driver offered his hand, but Degarius edged him aside and put his hands to her waist to steady her on the step. It was a trivial matter, who helped her from the step, but the strength in his hands made her feel as if she weighed nothing. Why was it that all her sacrifice had not brought her a fraction of the joy his calloused hands had? Had it been worth so little?

"Lord Degarius," the coachman called, "the snow's easing. Look ahead."

The flurrying snow faintly veiled a dark spire whose point disappeared into the low-slung clouds.

"The Worship Hall," Degarius said, and let go of her waist.

She had to tell him.

-❋-❋-❋-

"You did a fine job of driving," Degarius said as they settled in the coach. It seemed preferable to talk about anything other than what loomed just ahead.

"I had to use the Blue Eye."

"What?"

"This morning after you went down for coffee, that Gherian officer, the one with a missing eye, came in while I was dressing." Her hand went to the collar of her coat, to the place where the relic would be.

For all love! A guilt unlike anything he'd ever known, a pain worse than the slash that had scarred his chest, buckled him over. He bowed his head to his knees. Why had he left her? Into his snow-covered knees he asked, though he loathed to hear the answer, "What did he do?"

"He was going to blind me. I stopped him."

"He didn't touch you?"

"No. He's dead."

Degarius raised his head from his knees, but still unable to look at her, fixed his gaze out the frosty window. "I'm glad." Glad the bastard was dead. Glad she didn't show Kieran's misplaced contrition over the deed. Not yet. Who was he fooling? The ghosts never went away. Not even the ones who got what they deserved. The horror of what happened to her and what she had to do would follow her all her days. Or perhaps for only another handful of hours.

"But, the man in the hood, Alenius, he saw us," she said. "The soldier was wearing his uniform. He knows we are in Gheria. I should have told you sooner, but we can't stop."

Willing his captain's sensibilities to direct him, he said, "When we get nearer, get on the floor and cover yourself with a blanket."

"I'm sorry. Are you angry?"

"The soldier could have been anywhere in Gheria. Perhaps they'll think we are on the front." But Alenius would bet every one of his newly minted coins on them coming to the Fortress, Degarius knew. The guards would be waiting for them. For her.

A PRAYER FOR ABSOLUTION

Forbidden Fortress

T he coach ground to a crunching stop. The guards on the bridge spanning the river that ran around the Fortress had called for them to halt. They signaled out Degarius. Miss Nazar was on the floor, covered by a blanket. He closed the door quickly.

They didn't move to look inside, yet.

He'd always imagined triumphantly crossing this bridge as a general on horseback in company of a Sarapostan standard-bearer. Instead, here he was pretending to be a cabinetman waiting to be inspected by a pimply-faced guard and wondering how in the hell they'd ever get back out of the Fortress if they managed to get in. Lookouts dotted the ramparts. There was only one gate in the thick, high wall and it opened to this bridge over a river that hadn't frozen yet; the snow disappeared into its swirling dark current.

"Paper," the guard said.

Damn it. When did Gherians start carrying papers? Most couldn't read. The clan mark was standard identification. "What?"

"The invitation to the dinner in the Atrium. You're a cabinetman, aren't you?"

Thank goodness he hadn't yet volunteered himself as a cabinetman. The missing paper would've doomed them. "I'm here for the Solemnity."

"Come alone?" The guard glanced inside the coach.

"Marriage is one wrong I don't need to confess to the Eternal Master."

The guard laughed. "Show me your mark, then."

Degarius slipped his coat from his shoulders, loosened his collar, and bent forward so the purplish-blue prickling of a thistle on his neck showed.

The guard peered at the tattoo so long that Degarius began to feel uneasy. Had the old fellow who'd done it forgotten something? "The weather's breathing down my back," he said, hoping to sound like a great man irritated that a soldier should be thorough with him.

The guard let go of Degarius's shirt, but he had to wait, his head still bowed, while the guard shouted to a cohort of at least two dozen soldiers shivering and stomping through the snow at the foot of the bridge. Damn it. The guard wanted a superior's approval.

A man with a feather in his hat came and probed the tattoo with his gloved finger. "It's an old-style mark," he said. "Where do you come from?"

"Of course it's the old-style mark," Degarius said. "I'm an old man from near the border. It's the first time I've come for the Winter Solemnity. Look at the weather and treatment I get."

The feather-capped guard nodded. "You brought the weather with you from the south. Go on."

Degarius shouted to the driver, "Go directly to the Worship Hall," and climbed into the coach. They'd made it. Once inside the Worship Hall, hopefully no one would be on the lookout for her since they'd cleared the gate.

Once the carriage had passed beyond the wall and made it to the plaza before the Worship Hall, he peeled up the edge of the blanket. "It is safe to come out now."

She clambered to the seat.

"Getting to Alenius won't be as easy as we thought. We have to use the tunnels," he said. "The cabinetmen have special papers for the dinner."

"They found out you weren't a cabinetman and let you through?"

He recounted the exchange.

"And I was worried they'd find out you were a Sarapostan," she said.

He rubbed his gloves together, pleased that they'd made it through the gate. "I've been mistaken for a monk and a cabinetman, but no one has yet to mistake me for a Sarapostan." She smiled until he added, "Even you mistook me for a good man."

"I wasn't mistaken," she said.

"You're naive."

"Not anymore."

Thinking she referenced last night, the glimmer of good humor faded. "That alone should change your mind."

-❦-❦-❦-

His back to the wind whipping across the open plaza in front of the Worship Hall, Degarius slipped a purse into the driver's pocket. "Go to the livery and get me three excellent saddled horses." It was the only plan he could contrive. "Tie them with the coach. We might need to leave in a hurry." He turned to Miss Nazar. "Ready?"

He offered her his elbow to cross the patch of snow to one of the cleared paths leading to the Worship Hall's immense arched entry. She took it. How in all hell could he take her in? Yet, he kept walking until they joined the meager queue of pilgrims who'd braved the weather.

They passed through the arched door. Once inside, they were detained in a smallish entryway. The scent of a heavy, spicy incense coiled through the squeeze of people.

Were they checking people? Looking for a woman? She must be worried. He pressed his elbow to his side, giving her arm a squeeze of assurance. A gentle pressure returned the gesture as if she were reassuring him in return.

His glasses fogged and his coat made him uncomfortably warm. Reluctantly, he released her arm to take off his glasses. He opened his coat and cleared the lenses with a handkerchief. After putting them back on, he saw the reason they hadn't been allowed to enter. The pilgrims had paused for a procession of clerics wearing luxurious blue robes and carrying gold-framed portraits of the sovereigns. In pure, high voices, they chanted a litany of names. "The eunuchs are praying for the sovereign's ancestors," Degarius whispered in answer to Miss Nazar's questioning look. "Their breath is wasted on the last few rogues."

After the clerics passed, the pilgrims pressed into the main hall.

"Oh," Miss Nazar said. She was looking at the clerestory windows, yellow and clear prisms embedded in lacy black webs of lead and to the ceiling, a vaulted span painted the blue of the midday sky, but studded with gold-leaf stars in the pattern of the winter constellations. At the ceiling's center was a stylized sun circled by two rings of words. She pointed to it. "What does it say?"

"The outside rings say, 'To carry your spirit to spring, make it right with the Eternal Master before winter.' The inside says, 'Prayer does not change the One, it changes the one.' "

Something in her face changed. Her expression, so full of a yearning, cut to his core. It was the look he'd fallen in love with, the one that made him believe her words that he was a good man, that there was something redeemable in him. During their journey here, he hadn't seen it once. Had his anger blinded him? Or had she lost it, along with so many other things and only found it again, here. Maybe there was something redeemable in this place his ancestors built. Maybe at first it was only meant to inspire and give hope during the long Gherian winter. How could the Maker have let it be turned to such dark purposes as Lily Girls, eunuchs, and the raising of The Scyon? Or as Kieran would ask, how could the Gherians?

Degarius followed her gaze as it drifted down to a woman carefully holding a smoldering incense stick away from her grasping child as they made their way to the lines of curtained stalls set up for confessions. Something about the woman and child made his chest heat. Must the Maker throw in his face what was to be denied them?

"If we have time, I want to make a prayer," she said.

"Now?"

"A prayer for absolution, as the others make. It's what they're doing, isn't it?"

"What sins can you have?" he asked, incredulous. She *was* good. "Not the soldier at the inn."

"That wasn't of my choosing."

Then he remembered last night. Just as he suspected, she regretted it. Though he shouldn't have left in the morning, he didn't want to see the look of penance, didn't want to feel the blame for what happened between them. She hadn't looked at the mother and child with the same thoughts he had.

"Do we have time?" she asked, breaking into his bitter thought.

"A moment, since we don't have dinner plans."

Like the other pilgrims, she lit an incense stick from an oil lamp. Shielding her glowing stick from passersby's drafts, she peeked under curtains to find a vacant stall.

Degarius followed her visually. When she closed the curtain, he threaded through a pack of boys twiddling their fingers while cataloging their menial transgressions.

At the booths, a man left the partition next to Miss Nazar. He held the drapery open for Degarius.

Without knowing exactly why, Degarius entered and stood looming over the kneeler and the trough of spent incense. It was wrong to listen to an intensely private prayer, but he couldn't help himself. She was going to repent lying with him. He crossed his arms and thrust his hands in the fur sleeves of his coat.

Her voice carried through the thin wooden panel dividing them. In a steady litany, she spoke names of family and friends. She even asked for the health of the son of the Gherian general who'd stopped them at the crossroads. She mentioned Lerouge. She was actually praying for that bastard. Her voice dropped low, and Degarius strained to hear.

❈ ❈ ❈

"Those are my prayers. It was always easy to entrust others into your mercy. Yet, I stopped praying even those simple prayers after what happened to Solace. The words I spoke for Kieran's passing were said only by my lips, not by my heart. I stopped believing you had mercy for anyone. I forgot that your mercy is not for our bodies but for our souls. I forgot that prayer cannot change your already fully merciful heart, but changes ours, opens ours to mercy...and the gift of mercy that others give. I wholly gave you my youth, my heart, everything a girl had to give the one she loves. You were too big, too powerful for me to hurt. I thought you'd never leave me. Then, after I'd given you everything, I thought it was you who gave me the awful task with the Blue Eye and trial after trial with Chane. I stayed true to you through that, but you didn't bless me with the peace I'd sought for so long...and one by one, the few things in my small circle of life were taken from me. The kithara. Nan. The Solacians. And I loathed you as I loathed Allasan. I hated him leaving me alone to care for my dying father because he couldn't stomach the horror. I couldn't even dig the grave. I chipped at the frozen ground until the insides of my gloves soaked with blood. His body lay in the bed for three days until I had to bury him in the snow. Three days! Oh, Allasan. How could you leave me to that then return home and tell me that you couldn't stand the sight of me? How?

"Allasan, I am no better than you. I've never been. I couldn't forgive you as you couldn't forgive me."

✦–✦–✦

Her tortured voice trailed to nothing. Degarius burrowed his fingers under his hat and deep into his hair. His dear Ari.

✦–✦–✦

"Yet here, Maker, I've finally heard your invitation for me to return to you. In the beauty of this place, I felt you tug at my heart. It wasn't you who put the task of the Blue Eye upon me or took the kithara. It was the superior. It wasn't you who murdered the Solacians. It was Alenius. It wasn't you who took Nan from me. That was doomed from the start because of who we were. Forgive me. You gave me the fortitude to endure what Allasan could not. What a mercy that was! All along, my trials have been of my own making. All along, you have given me permission to serve you without bitterness, but I kept my anger inside so long to punish myself, to punish Allasan. And it only made my soul a black, displeasing thing. I'm afraid soon my life will end, and I'll have given you nothing worthy in return for it. Now, I send my prayer on this sweet smoke in hope that my life, as it burns away like the incense, will send up something pleasing. How am I to serve you? It isn't this task with the Blue Eye. You'd not ask anyone to take the lives of others in order to be your shacra. I do this because men have given me no choice.

"Once, I thought I could serve you as a Solacian. Then I dared hoped being a wife would be noble. I was foolish, hoping that despite everything, Nan loved me as I love him. My stubborn heart is your gift to me, but I keep using it to cling to those things that bring me sorrow. It won't let Nan go. Forgive me for trying last night to make my time with him something it wasn't. I must be grateful for what he is—courageous. Is there nothing he fears? I know he won't leave me to this task alone. He is no Payter or Allasan, and it gives me peace, faith, to know that your goodness exists not just in death, but here among us. It is why I loved him from the start."

⸻ ⸻ ⸻

Degarius threw aside the curtain. Arms swinging, he plowed through the tittering boys, hardly noting how they jumped from his path. Her confession was reverberating in his head. He slumped against a pillar and turned his gaze to the vast blue ceiling. He knew exactly how she was meant to serve the Maker. Why had he given her the ring through a servant? Why hadn't he told her the truth last night or this morning? For the same damn reason he couldn't tell her now. He wasn't courageous.

When Ari rejoined him, she brought one of the oil lamps the penitents used to light incense. He peeled from the pillar. She wasn't teary-eyed. Holding up the lamp, she said with a strange lightness in her voice, "Maker forgive me, I pilfered it. I thought we'd need it." She nodded to a row of low arches on the other side of the Worship Hall. "Lina said it's the door under the dove window."

"You *are* good."

"For taking a lamp?" A false note of humor sounded in her voice.

"You could have had nothing to confess. You are good."

She lowered the lamp. Her eyes glinted with its light, and in the same tenuous yet playful voice she said, "You don't know me."

His heart lurched. Through her onionskin-thin layer of mirth, he saw that she was trying not to be afraid. He half smiled. "I know you well enough."

"I wish there were more people," she said. "We are obvious standing here. The dove door?"

He bowed and motioned her to lead.

They reached the room without seeming to attract notice. He put his hand upon the knob and held his breath that it wasn't locked.

It turned.

Lina had written that the clerics used the room to store incense and vestments. This room was an office, richly furnished with dark, heavy furniture and a rabian rug. But, just as Lina described, Gherian words were carved into a waist-height band of lighter-colored stone that ran around the room. Perhaps it was foolish to imagine the room wouldn't have changed purpose in the passing years.

They began to look for the word *descend*.

"Is this it?" Miss Nazar pointed to the set of symbols she'd memorized. It was on the panel behind the desk. She set the lantern down, laid her palm flat against the word, and pushed. A section of the wall pivoted open. The hatch was wooden but cleverly veneered with thin plates of stone to match the wall. It opened to a dark space.

The door to the room creaked.

WINTER GARDEN

Degarius bowed to the cleric, who by his ermine-trimmed robes was high-ranking. "Venerated sir, I wished a private word with the lady. It's impossible in the hall."

The cleric's chin disappeared into his thick, pink neck. "This isn't a public room." His voice was high and thin for a portly man. "It's my office."

Ari had straightened. She was trying to nudge the door to the tunnel closed with her foot.

The cleric shifted his bulk under his robes and glanced to the lamp and Ari. His eyelids slitted over his bulging eyes. He saw the open door to the tunnel. He began to draw his hulking chest up, as if to gather breath to bellow for the guards.

Degarius slipped his hand into his coat for his knife. Ari noted. Good. He gave the tiniest nod to the lamp. *Just pick it up, Ari. Distract him.* She bent to pick up the lamp. The cleric's lips parted.

Degarius drew his knife, darted behind him, and held the edge to his neck. "Don't yell."

The cleric's neck jiggled against the blade as he shook his head. Degarius debated killing him now or using him to lead them in the tunnels. The clerics had blindfolded Lina when they brought her through. There could be an endless underground maze beneath the Forbidden Fortress for all he knew. In the cleric's ear, Degarius said in Gherian, "Take us to the atrium, and I'll spare you."

The cleric trembled. "Why?"

"Yes or no. I don't mind killing you." Degarius lightly drew the blade across the cleric's sagging chin. "Ari, turn around. I don't want you to see this."

"I'll take you," the cleric gasped.

Degarius drew his sword and held it to the cleric's back. "Try anything and I run you through." To Ari he said in Anglish, "Take my knife and the lantern."

Hearing the Anglish, the cleric looked pleadingly to Ari and said in Anglish so she'd understand, "I'm a holy man."

"Then you'll help us," Ari said.

Degarius pushed him toward the stair. "Go on, holy man."

They descended a steep narrow stair to a passageway that smelled of dank soil. It snaked for long a distance, the length of the Worship Hall grounds, Degarius guessed, without exits or converging corridors. He counted another 358 paces until they reached two openings to the left and one going right. "Where do they lead?"

The cleric pointed to the right tunnel. "That one goes to the armory and farther along, the docks. The first left goes to the queen's house, the second to the Lily Girl dormitory and the palace."

The explanation seemed to match Lina's description of the Forbidden Fortress's layout. Degarius pointed his sword to the second left. The atrium was in the palace.

The floor sloped steadily upward, but the ceiling didn't. By the time they came to a door sealing the tunnel, they were crouching. Lina said there'd be a door. The cleric opened it. The tunnels were emergency escapes so they were kept unlocked. Clerics escorted the Lily Girls everywhere; there was no danger of them escaping.

Degarius paused to listen for footsteps in this more frequented section of the tunnel. It was quiet.

The cleric waved them along. "There." He pointed to a ladder. "It goes to the pump room for the fountains in the atrium."

Degarius stopped to consider. Lina said there was a ladder to the atrium. Her maps showed it being farther from the door, though. Maybe she hadn't drawn the map quite to scale. "I'm going to look. Ari, keep the knife on our holy man." He climbed the short ladder to an overhead door. He nudged open the hatch. The room above was dark and quiet. He opened the hatch, climbed through, then knelt with his sword pointed at the cleric's neck as the cleric scaled the ladder. Ari followed with the light. Tubing and pumps filled the small room. "Why aren't they manned and running?"

"Not during the Solemnity," answered the cleric.

Degarius cracked the door to the atrium ajar. In floated a snowflake. What in all hell? This wasn't the atrium.

"Spies!" the cleric screeched.

A hard blow hit Degarius in the center of the back. He flew forward through the door and landed facedown in the snow. He looked up. Everything in the distance was a blur. His glasses were gone.

Moaning, low and deep, as if it came from the very earth, resonated through his ears and body.

Ari screamed.

A boot smashed into the wrist of Degarius's sword hand. Two Gherian guards stood over him. A half dozen more were steps away.

❦ ❦ ❦

The cleric grabbed Arvana's arms and shoved her backward into the pump-house wall. His weight pinned her hands and the knife behind her back. She twisted against him, but he was too heavy. She arched her back and freed her hand with the knife, but he caught it, slammed it to the wall, and pressed harder against her. "You said you were a holy man," she pleaded.

"I am." With his free hand, he raked the front of her dress. His fingers caught on the Blue Eye, and he pulled. Her neck burned as the chain dug into her flesh before it snapped.

The cleric spat into her face, and in heavily accented Anglish said, "Sovereign Alenius promised me this. Thank you for bringing it straight to me. I will be his holy Judge." He laughed.

As his belly heaved, she ripped her knife hand free and plunged the blade into his neck.

The cleric reeled backward, the knife still in his throat. He ran into a pump and pitched over it.

She lunged for his hand, for the Blue Eye, but a soldier jumped before her. Another came at her from the side and threw his arms around her. She thrashed wildly against him, but he lifted her from her feet and carried her from the pump house.

❈ ❈ ❈

Every time Degarius tried to get to his knees, the soldiers kicked him down. He didn't feel their boots. He had to get up. A black boot flashed toward his face. He squeezed his eyes closed and curled his head between his arms. The boot caught his shoulder.

"Stop," a voice yelled. "Get up."

Degarius got to all fours and looked up. A blade, Assaea, was pointed right between his eyes. Some bastard had it. As Degarius slowly unbent and came to his feet, another soldier grabbed his arms, locked his elbows behind his back, and pushed him toward a Gherian Fortress Guard commander. The commander's breath steamed over Degarius's face as he asked, "A spy, are you? I'm a gracious man. I'll show you what you came here to see." He cracked an ugly smile and nodded to his left. "And some things you didn't come here to see."

Degarius looked to where the commander nodded. Two soldiers held Ari.

The earth rumbled again. The soldiers holding him tensed and glanced to their commander.

"Megreth doesn't like you and neither do I," the commander said. He walked to Ari and shoved his hand under her coat. "But I like her."

"Don't touch her," Degarius growled.

The commander ran his hand up her bodice to her chest. She wrenched against her captors, but they pulled her arms tighter. The commander curled his fingers up under Degarius's mother's necklace. "This looks worth my trouble." He ripped it from her neck.

Degarius squinted. Where was the Blue Eye? Had the damn cleric taken it from her?

The commander threw the necklace to a soldier, then curtly turned away from Ari and signaled the soldiers to follow him.

They were in some kind of garden. Snow filled in the fountain and covered brown tangles of vines that crawled the high walls. The soldiers led them around a row of white cedars to what appeared to have once been a huge reflecting pool. A grid of metal bars crisscrossed the pool's surface and an elaborate pulley system was rigged to open a trap-door-style hatch. Heat waves distorted the air over the pool and melted the snow midair. No snow stuck to the ground around the pool.

A soldier opened a hamper and lugged out a man's head. Another worked the pulley to open the hatch.

"Watch closely," the commander, said. "Alenius will order the same to be your fate."

The soldiers pushed them to the edge of the pool. It had been dug out. At the bottom of the pit was the draeden that had destroyed Solace.

The commander shouted, "Wakeup, wakeup," at the creature. "Time for a snack."

The draeden's eyelids peeled opened. Its irises were a pulsing red, as if gushing with blood. Instead of going for the man's head, it beat its constrained wings against the grate roof and stone sides of the grotto. Its snout rammed the bars closest to the soldier keeping Assaca. Did it sense his sword?

"Aren't you afraid?" the commander asked Ari. When she didn't reply, he shouted at her, "Are you deaf that you don't answer me? I'll make our haughty lady sufficiently humble to go before the sovereign." He wrested her arms from the soldiers holding her and shoved her onto her back in the snow. Frantically digging her heels into the snow, she tried to scramble away, but the soldiers swooped around her, grabbing her arms and legs. The commander threw a wicked grin at Degarius and said to the men holding him, "If our spy looks away, gouge out his eyes."

The commander pulled her dress up. "Riding breeches?"

Ari tried to kick him, but the soldier who had her legs pressed all his weight into them. She cried a wordless noise that was angry, defiant, and frightened all at once. The commander tore at the breeches.

A powerful urge in Degarius's gut told him to spring like an animal, to lash out in mad, indiscriminate violence to gain her a moment more by drawing the attention to him, but twenty years of discipline tempered him. He snapped his head back into the nose of the soldier holding him, yanked his arms free, then turned around and swept his foot under the guard, sending him down. The guard with Assaea came rushing, ready to lop off Degarius's head. Degarius ducked, grabbed the guard's leg, and pulled it out from under him. As the guard started to fall, Degarius twisted his leg. The guard landed facedown and lost his grip on Assaea. Degarius snatched his sword and, finally giving into his rage, slashed furiously in a wide circle.

The scraping sound of metal grating against rock stopped everyone. The soldiers gawked as the bolts attaching the metal grid to the fountain wall popped.

"Hold the grate down," the commander screamed as he got up from his knees and off of Ari. "It's trying to get out."

The soldiers rushed the grate and threw their weight upon its edges.

The draeden sunk to the bottom and the grate settled back onto the wall. The men let out a nervous, relieved cheer.

With a thunderous *boom*, the grate flew into the air, taking with it the men who'd been holding it down. The draeden, with its wings closed tight against its body, had launched upward.

❀ ❀ ❀

Hot air wafted over Arvana. The commander pulled her to her feet. She made a desperate lurch to the side. She had to get away, had to find the Blue Eye. He grabbed her arms and pushed her toward the pit. Planting her feet, she tried to stand her ground, but her shoes slid in the mud from where the draeden's heat had melted the snow. He shoved her harder. She teetered backward.

Suddenly, Nan was behind the commander. He raised his sword.

Arvana flinched. The commander shrieked, let go of her, and his body collapsed at her feet. From behind her came a loud ruffling sound.

"Run!" Nan clasped her hand and tugged her to jump over the dead body.

She glanced backward as they raced to the pump house. The draeden, rising up to full stature, was opening its wings. It dwarfed the trees. White circles appeared around its eyes.

Heat flashed against her back. The trees burst into flame.

They were at the pump-house door.

The draeden's head crashed through the burning trees.

She opened the door and darted inside. Nan had just crossed the threshold when a column of flame jetted past.

The Blue Eye. She bent beside the dead cleric and found his stiff hand. The relic wasn't there. It had to be here. She rifled through the folds of his robes. Nothing. The floor. She clawed the dirt. Nothing. "It has to be here." Her glance darted to the pumps. A chain hung over a section of tubing. No relic. She raked the floor beneath the tube. There! She clutched it in her palm. "I have it." She grabbed the lamp and dropped into the tunnel. Nan was behind her.

To the left was the section of tunnel they'd already traveled. It led back to the Worship Hall. Their errand didn't lay in that direction.

A blast, like a thousand pieces of wood splintering, exploded overhead. The draeden must have sheered away the pump house. Evening light filtered into the tunnel, and then it went dark again.

They ran to the right.

The tunnel shook with a roar, like a wave crashing the shore but a hundred times louder. Bits of mortar dropped from the tunnel ceiling. A shower of dirt obscured the meager lamplight. Lina's map flashed into Arvana's memory. They had to keep going straight to get to the atrium.

Another roar. Ahead, a stone fell from the ceiling. And another. The tunnel was collapsing. They had to get out. A darker area loomed to the right. This tunnel led to Alenius's bedchamber. As they turned into it, a flame shot through the corridor where they'd been. The draeden had its snout down that tunnel. There was no going back that way, even if it led to the atrium.

They ran deeper into the tunnel. Another flame lit the corridor they'd left. They were safe, for the moment. The draeden was far too huge to get actually into the tunnels. Arvana paused to collect her breath. She held up the lantern. Nan's glasses were gone. He was squinting at her.

He nodded to her hand that clutched the relic. "Do you think the cleric opened it?"

"No."

He smiled and laughed in deep relief. "Maybe we still have some surprise on our side."

A gloominess darker than the tunnel's shadowed her voice when she had to tell him, "The cleric knew who I was."

"For all love—"

The tunnel rumbled again and pea-sized chunks of mortar rained into her hat. The draeden might not be able to fit into the tunnel, but it was determined to destroy them. They had to get out.

Not far ahead was a well-worn flight of wooden steps instead of a ladder.

Atop the step was a white door with a gold doorknob.

A cleric crawled from under the stairs. He had a knife.

A TERRIBLE MERCY

Degarius approached the knife-waving cleric, a boy in plain blue robes who reeked of onion. He was so slender that taking him would be like swinging a scythe through a single stalk of wheat. It was against the little bit of morality Degarius figured he had left to kill or wound such a boy, but if he didn't relinquish the knife, there was no choice. He raised his sword and kept his voice low in case someone was in the bedchamber on the other side of the door. "If you drop the knife and let us pass I won't harm you."

The boy stopped waving the knife but still clenched it in his fist. With the same frantic desperation with which he waved the knife, he looked at Ari and said, "You're the Judge they said was coming."

Damn it. Evidently all the eunuchs were expecting her. "Drop the knife. Now."

Smoke began to choke the tunnel.

"Don't judge me. Not yet. Let me make absolution." The boy raised his chin and rolled his gaze to the close ceiling of the tunnel.

"No, I—" Ari cried, but the blade was slicing across his throat.

Degarius turned and took the hand that covered her horror-stricken mouth.

"I'm not a Judge," she said, not to the boy who was slumping to the floor, but to him.

You're Paulus, a shacra. He pulled her after him up the stairs.

The door with the gold knob flew open and Degarius, with sword poised, charged into a chamber walled with mirrors. An elderly cleric holding a metal candlestick stood beside a bed draped with diaphanous gold curtains. For all love, first a boy and now an old man. But it wasn't the time for scruples. A single thrust of Assaea dispatched the cleric.

A gasp came from inside the shrouded bed. Degarius threw the curtain aside. A Lily Girl, her blonde, waist-length hair beaded with sapphires, was sitting up in the bed and hiding her face behind her crossed arms. Between sobs she said, "You're not supposed to see me. Kill me. Please."

Degarius shook his head and thought of his grandmother. She must have wept in this room.

The Lily Girl lowered her arms. Tears ran pink rivers into her white-powdered face. She gave a pleading look to Ari. "Lady, please help me. I'm a chosen one. I don't want to carry a monster inside of me."

The floor rumbled.

Degarius's blood went cold. It was as the Solacian superior said. Draeden were born of girls—Lily Girls. The elderly cleric was making sure the girl would perform her wretched duty. Any scruple Degarius had in killing him was relieved. Alenius was going to be next. There was no justice too brutal to compensate for what Alenius had done to his grandmother, her family, to what he would do to this girl.

In clumsy but intelligible Gherian Ari told the Lily, "I won't let that happen."

"Do you know how to get to the atrium?" Degarius asked the Lily.

"Go right outside this door. Straight all the way down the hall. Then right...no." A panicked shadow crossed her face. Her lips trembled. She was going to cry again.

Ari removed her coat and gave it to the girl. "Put it on." The Lily looked confused, but did as she was told. Ari then took off her hat. She pressed the hat into the girl's hands and motioned her to tuck her braided hair under it.

The girl put on the hat and Ari began shoving braids up into the deep crown. "Tell her she has to show us how to get to the atrium, and then she must leave the palace right away, find our coachman waiting before the Worship Hall, and tell him Lord Degarius said to take care of her."

He hesitated. Not because he, or his coachman, wouldn't take care of the girl, but because Ari had given up her coat and hat. Either it was a noble act of mercy or she didn't expect to need them.

"Nan, tell her."

It was an act of kindness, he decided as he spoke Ari's words to the girl. He couldn't step into the hall thinking otherwise.

The Lily rubbed her eyes, smudging pink circles into the death-pale powder.

"Give me your handkerchief, Nan."

Ari dabbed his handkerchief to her tongue and wiped the remaining powder from the girl's face.

Degarius listened at the door. It was quiet. "Let's go." To the Lily he said, "Take me to the atrium, and then remember what I said."

The Lily Girl led them through a maze of hallways to a double set of heavy doors guarded by two sentries who, with suspicion, watched them approach.

"Halt!"

"Look at us!" Degarius shouted and shook a fist while he eased his other hand inside his coat for his sword. "It's chaos out there. Look what happened to me—a cabinetman. Look what happened to my wife. To my daughter. Why aren't you doing something?"

While the sentries looked at Ari's filthy ripped dress, the tearful girl in the fur coat, and each other in confusion, Degarius, in one swift move, drew his sword and slashed it across their necks. For a stunned moment, they remained standing, their eyes wide circles of terror. Degarius shoved them out of the way and they collapsed against the wall. The Lily Girl's hands flew to cover her eyes. Without his bidding, Ari grabbed the Lily's elbow. Thank the Maker, Ari kept her wits about her.

Degarius cracked the door. It was nearly sunset so the vestibule outside was crowded to the edges with cabinetmen and their wives who were waiting to enter the atrium for dinner and to hear the declaration of war. They were murmuring anxiously to one another as a regiment of soldiers came thundering through. The soldiers were probably leaving the atrium to help subdue the draeden, but the cabinetmen didn't seem to know what was happening.

The three of them couldn't just walk out into the vestibule. Covered with dirt, they looked like they'd been through hell. Ari had the Blue Eye. She *could* take them all. Degarius didn't want that, though, not if he could help it. "Ari," he whispered, "I'm going to try to create a diversion to get rid of the cabinetmen."

She nodded.

He opened the door, stepped into the vestibule, and shouted, "Countrymen, follow the guards. The Worship Hall is on fire. It was Sarapostans. We need all hands."

The cabinetmen poured toward the exit, but some of their wives lingered.

"You, too," Degarius shouted at the women. "Because of your fine dresses will you stand here while the hall burns?"

Shamed, they followed their husbands.

"Go," Ari said and nudged the Lily Girl to join the women.

The thought flashed to Degarius that if someone had been so kind to his grandmother, none of this would have happened. He held his hand to Ari. She took it. Together they waited for the vestibule to clear. How thin and soft her hand was. It was the farthest thing on earth from a warrior's hand. She wasn't going to fight The Scyon with her hands, though. It would be soul-to-soul combat. Her spirit was deep and good, enduring of trials, and steadfast. After everything that had happened, she still loved the Maker, still loved him. Some might call that foolishness. But he understood it. In any battle, against any odds, he'd keep swinging his sword. She held onto her love as tightly as he held his cause. Perhaps there was no one better to have the Blue Eye. Perhaps The Scyon feared no one more than a Maker's woman.

A line of guards remained before the atrium door.

"I can't take them all," Degarius whispered. "They're soldiers. They accepted their fate. Understand?"

"What do you want?" an atrium guard asked.

Ari squeezed his hand, then let go.

JOLE, YEAR 0

Arvana pressed the latch, the Blue Eye sprang open, and she gazed into it. Her spirit compressed to cross through the relic into Hell, but it was a discomfort instead of agony. Hell's bitter smell was so familiar she didn't flinch at it. She looked up. Nan's spirit burned bright, and Assaea gleamed even brighter. Lina's soul drifted from the sword's protective glow.

"I remember this dress." Lina's ghostly hands passed through the rent and soiled fabric of Arvana's dress. "But you've ruined it."

"We don't have time." Arvana checked the locket. The Scyon was glaring at her through the eye slits in his black head covering. In the background was a sapphire-encrusted throne.

Lina, who was looking into the locket from over Arvana's shoulder, said, "That throne is in the atrium. I remember it. Are you close?"

On the other side of the door. They just had to get through it. Holding the open Blue Eye in her palm, Arvana willed the soldiers' souls to her. Their life threads spun through the Blue Eye. The guards collapsed. The Blue Eye grew warm in her hand with the number of spirits crowding through it. Having passed through, they reappeared before her as shades, the light of their lives ebbing from them.

The body of a guard writhed before her. As she stepped around him, a sick feeling crept up her throat. Even if she returned his soul to life, he'd be damaged, never himself again.

Nan wedged his shoulder to the atrium door and pushed. It opened freely.

She held the locket ready as she entered a vast room lit by a hundred candles, hung with blue Gherian flags, and set with dozens of tables laid with gold plate for the cabinetmen. The aroma of roasted meat filled the air. Four stories up, an astounding metal-and-glass roof, grayed by snow and dusk, capped the space. Together, Nan and she walked through the tables to the far end of the room toward a gold-and-blue curtained pavilion with a polished metal roof.

The curtain parted and a man, wearing white gloves and the finest blue robes trimmed in white fur and beaded with sapphires, stepped out. An immense aura of otherworldly glittering, silvery light surrounded him. His life aura was different than any Arvana had ever seen. A silky, dark blue hood covered his face. Arvana had seen the hood in the Blue Eye. "Nan, he's—" She began to say he was The Scyon, but the hooded man began to speak in an oddly beautiful, warm and soothing voice.

"So, you're alive...the Sarapostan who took my little one from the lake and the Maker's woman who bears the Blue Eye. It is fitting that you shall both be the first to behold the Lord of the Hants, the Divine Sovereign." He walked to edge of the dais. No, he didn't walk. He was so graceful he seemed to glide.

The Scyon hooked his thumbs beneath the bottom of the hood. Fear pricked Arvana. What kind of monster would he be?

The fabric rose from the face of a young Gherian with fine, clear skin and thick blond hair that fell in waves around his high cheeks. There was a feminine beauty about him. His eyes, the same blue as Nan's, set their sight on her. They were mesmerizing.

"It is a beautiful form, isn't it?" The young Gherian caressed his own cheek. "Even the Maker has not created such perfection, for time has no toll upon the living flesh we have wrought. We are a god. We will never grow old or infirm. We will never die. Our offspring will bring peace to the ends of the world. There will be no hunger or need. Is not peace what you want? But peace never comes without sacrifice. Isn't that right, Maker's woman? Oh, there will be days of war, but this time it will be different. Give me the Blue Eye. Give me Paulus's sword. Lukis and Paulus did not bring peace, only more war as men scrabbled for power and wealth. They were not saviors."

Arvana shook her head. "You aren't a god or a savior. In the Maker is the possibility of all things. We are free to love the Maker, or be indifferent. You will send the draeden after all who won't worship you. You only offer peace for the glory it brings you. You aren't a savior."

❦ ❦ ❦

What in the hell was going on? Who was this imposter who'd worn the hood? Alenius was a bald old man, at least seventy-five, and this boy was no supernatural monster. "Tell me where Alenius is, where The Scyon is, or I'll kill you," Degarius said.

"We are Alenius and Breena. We are the divine sovereign, the saviors. There is no Scyon."

"Like hell you're Alenius." Degarius hurtled to the dais and poised his sword to slice the young man's neck. "Tell me."

"I knew you would not give me the Blue Eye or sword, but I knew you were stupid enough to listen." He raised one arm and pointed a finger upward.

Degarius felt Ari grab his coat and pull it. Breaking glass shattered the silence. The roof was collapsing.

"Get under a table," she screamed.

He turned. She was scrambling under a table. He dove after her. Giant panes of the atrium's glass roof and pieces of metal crashed around them. He turned on his side, threw his arm over her and drew her close so his chest shielded her head.

A heavy, dull *thud* shuddered the table. The blanket of snow from the roof had fallen on it. The sound of a flag lashing in the wind, except louder, whooshed through the room. The snow that had fallen from the roof whipped in a blizzard-like frenzy. Degarius's face stung from the pelting ice crystals.

When the snow settled, he peered from under the table. Flakes drifted down from the open roof. Across the room, two massive, black feet with claws that burned a deep orange color like a smoldering coal, stood amid the roof's wreckage.

The draeden.

The bottoms of its wings, darkly translucent like a fish fin, folded up.

❖ ❖ ❖

Arvana uncurled from Nan. Her vision flickered between this world and the next. Lina hovered near Nan. The table oddly bisected her spirit. Arvana shook the image from her head and got to her hands and knees, like Nan, under the table. The draeden's neck bent toward them and routed its snout under the table edge. Arvana's pulse tripped. The creature's hide around its nose glowed red. The air waved with heat. It could incinerate them. She had to draw it into Hell. Where was its soul? No aura surrounded it. Arvana glanced at her palm to the open Blue Eye. Assaea gleamed with otherworldly light and the golden aura of life surrounded Nan; the relic was working. Dear Maker, how could the Blue Eye be useless against the draeden?

Assaea flashed. Nan jabbed at the draeden's snout. The blade sliced the flaring edge of the creature's nostril. The draeden reared and heaved the table across the room.

A gold tendril snaked from the wounded snout.

"Nan, do you see that?"

He squinted hard. "What?"

It was the draeden's soul; its body simply encased it. Deep within her chest, Arvana set her will, hard and fierce, against the draeden. The tendril of spirit wove toward the Blue Eye, but it grew thinner as the wound on the draeden's snout closed, the flesh knitting before their eyes. When the wound fully closed, the bit of spirit that had reached the Blue Eye turned to a wisp of smoke and floated back to the draeden, who was breathing it in. Nan would have to deal the draeden a terrible wound in order for it to lose enough spirit to die before the injury healed. Perhaps she could hasten the leaking of the spirit. Draw it out. Lina could help. "Lina, we have to engage that spirit."

Lina shook her head. "I can't leave the blessed light. I will fade."

"Being *always* alone isn't a blessing. It's a curse."

"I know," Nan said grimly.

Arvana hadn't realized she'd spoken aloud.

Nan held his sword ready, his narrowed eyes fixed on the draeden. It coiled its neck to the side and looked at them askance, as if planning its next strike. In the open, they were easy targets.

A tangled heap of metal lay to the right. "Nan," she whispered and gestured to the wreckage. He nodded. In a crouched run, she headed for the debris. It wasn't much cover, but would keep the creature from getting right to them. Her boots crunched through the snow. Shards of glass were everywhere. Would Nan see them? "Stay behind me."

From the corner of her eye, she saw the draeden move.

They reached the pile of twisted metal, and the draeden was on the other side, arching its neck up and over the wreckage. It opened its mouth, filled with rows of spiky, yellow teeth.

Nan stood tall with poised sword. The draeden turned its head and swooped it down to take him in its jaws. Nan skirted to the side and swung his sword at the exposed underside of the jaw. His blade slashed through the soft tissues.

Spirit and blood streamed from the wound. Arvana grabbed the ethereal tendril with her free hand. It wrapped around her forearm, coiled her elbow, and slithered to her shoulder. She backed violently away.

The tendril wrapped Arvana's neck. She knew she should pull the tendril away, but the Blue Eye was in her free hand and she couldn't drop it A spirit couldn't kill her. It couldn't hurt her body. Physically, there was no pain or choking, but why did she feel so languid, as if in bed, just awakened and unwilling to be aroused?

"Let go of Willow!" Chane's spirit, a tangle of dull, gray desiccated life-threads, flew at the draeden with all the uncompromising authority he'd had in life, and began to wrench the coils. "Get away," he shouted at Arvana as he loosened the coil around her neck.

Arvana dropped. The moment she was free from the coils, her spirit seemed to expand with great force and vigor as if it had been smothered and was now taking a deep, reviving breath. She edged backward from the metal tangle through the snow. The draeden's head hovered for a moment, caught in indecision of whether to attack Nan, her, or recoil its soul from Chane. In its moment of consideration, Nan hacked its long neck.

The draeden's open mouth barreled toward Nan.

He leaped away, pivoted, and brought his sword down into its skull.

Spirit gushed out.

"I vowed to defeat you," Chane shouted and flung himself into the new tendrils of the draeden's soul as they passed through the Blue Eye. They twisted around him like thread on a spool. The creature moaned and Chane's agonized screams, so like her father's in his last days, made Arvana want to do anything quiet them. Oh, the horrible things she had considered doing to her father.

Nan brought his sword down again and again, hacking the draeden's flesh.

The Blue Eye flashed and in Hell, Arvana saw Chane cocooned by the draeden's writhing coils. Chane's screams grew muffled, then stopped. It seemed impossible that his spirit, so strong in both anger and righteousness, had been finally subdued.

Then, bright bits of light, like sparks from a flint, flew from the cocooning shroud of the draeden's spirit. These bits of light joined into a brilliant sphere. Though it bore no resemblance to Chane, Arvana knew it was he, as one's body knows it is daylight before the eyes open from sleep. His valor and suffering had transformed him. The sphere of light grew small, kept concentrating until with a final flash it disappeared. There was something, someplace beyond Hell.

The draeden's body lurched forward and collapsed onto the pile of metal and glass that groaned and crackled with the impact.

As when Nan had killed the poison draeden, a foul wind whipped from the creature's spirit fully entering Hell. The tendril that had held Chane turned a dead gray color and rejoined with the rest of the draeden's spirit in a spinning vortex that snatched up millions of spirits with its power. Out of the vortex's center came a spirit image of the draeden. In life, the creature's carcass was a steaming heap of flesh.

Nan, his hand to his hip and his face red with exhaustion, stood catching his breath.

"No!" a shrill voice cut through the air. It was Alenius. He stood before the pavilion. Its roof had collapsed and its curtains were sheered away, revealing the throne, a massive table turned on its side, and a box with a glass top that had been shattered. Alenius's gloved hands picked away pieces of glass from the box. He reached inside and was stroking or petting whatever was in it. "Breena, don't do this. The people will finally love me," he mumbled as if to himself. "My power will bring peace. We will be the saviors. Breena, I gave you life within me. We are soul mates, finally husband

and wife. Don't you love me? You know I tried to
bring you back with the Beckoner, but your body
was too ruined. Isn't it better this way? Otherwise,
I would have died of age. We will be together
always." He jerked his hand from the box and
gripped the front of his robe and his voice went
higher pitched, as if it were a woman speaking,
"You've always been a fool, Alenius. The power is
mine and so is your life."

He ripped his robe open and cast it off. His arms
and torso were perfectly muscled, but there was
something ghastly wrong with his chest. On the
side where his heart should be, the skin stretched
over an egg-shaped mound. With one heave, he
pushed the box with the broken glass top from its
pedestal. It crashed to its side and a corpse fell
partially out. The body was wrapped in a woman's
robes, but they were cut up the back and had fallen
away to reveal a skeleton with pads for flesh. Its
blonde wig was half off the skull and the nose of a
wax mask was gone. "You have broken your
promise, Alenius, as I knew you would," the voice
screeched. "You can't deliver the world to me."
The round muscles on his arms and chest began to
shrivel, his hair shed from his scalp, and the skin on
his face sagged into an old man's wrinkles.

A feeble voice came from the man's withered
lips. "I was divine, the ruler—"

"The ruler of nothing," said the other voice. The beautiful silver aura around Alenius lost its luster and became pale green, the color of frozen pond water. The flesh around the egg shape turned dark purple. The skin over Alenius's body split and peeled. The flesh beneath was blackened, as if it had been charred. The Gherian features sloughed from his face, leaving an open nasal cavity and a lipless mouth. As if every blood vessel in them had ruptured, the whites of his eyes went red. The egg shape could only be the Beckoner, the relic that brought death to life.

On one hand and knees, Arvana held out the Blue Eye. So Alenius had tried to bring back to life the body of a dead lover named Breena, but failed, so shared his own body with her. Breena was what the ancients called The Scyon. Arvana willed The Scyon's pale green aura to her, but like the draeden's, it would not come. "Nan, you must wound it," she called.

Nan was already flying toward The Scyon. It cowered and crossed its arms over its face. Thank the Maker it was once a woman, unused to the threat of the blade.

The instant Assaea touched the blackened flesh, the Beckoner in The Scyon's chest lit up brighter than a moon seen through a spyglass. A crackling light bolted from the creature's chest. It flashed to Nan, burst, and he flew backward into a table crisscrossed by a twisted section of the roof's metal framework. He hit the table with the back of his legs and flailed onto it. Dear Maker, had one of the jagged lengths of metal pierced him? He groaned, but by some miracle, he curled his torso and slid to his feet. He'd landed between the beams. He took a step, but his hand went to his chest where the flash struck him, and he faltered. There was a black, burned spot on his coat and a gray area deadened a part of the splendid golden aura of his life.

The egg in The Scyon's chest again grew bright.

"Don't hurt him," Arvana cried and rose. She held out the Blue Eye, and from the wound in the creature's side sucked a huge portion of the icy-green spirit into it. In Hell, The Scyon's spirit separated into long, thin frozen blades of sharp, serrated cord grass. They lashed at Arvana's soul's hands, covering them with thousands of small, wickedly burning cuts. From each cut ran a rivulet of spirit, each carrying a small portion of the reservoir of loneliness in her soul.

She was a small girl wearing her favorite frock, the one with yellow flowers embroidered on the hem. She'd wandered into the tall grass on the far side of the pasture. In the wind, the tops of the grass wavered over her head. The more she tried to find her way out of it, the deeper into the dense blades she seemed to be. They nicked her arms with stinging cuts. She'd shouted and shouted until her throat was sore, but no one came. The sun was setting and the hum of a million insects was rising. She curled in the grass, her knees drawn up under the frock, and gave over to crying. Then she heard her mother call her name. She jumped up. "Mama! Mama!"

"Ari?"

"Mama!"

Finally, the grass parted, and she reached to be plucked from the terrible grass. Her mother yanked Ari's outstretched hand and in a shrill voice said, "What did I tell you? Never go in the grass. I'll have your father whip you for it." Ari cowered and pulled away her hand. Her mother became all the shriller, yelling for her to quit crying and to come along.

Arvana looked up. She'd let go of The Scyon's spirit. Claws erupted from its white gloves, and then expanding flesh burst through the fabric. Its limbs elongated, and it grew taller until it seemed an immense skeleton covered in skin the color of burned paper. The creature in the world was doubly large now and wings had sprouted from its back.

The spirit shot toward her hand and through the Blue Eye, but when it came out in Hell, it took the form of a shard of gray ice and flew at her. She cowered into a ball, but the shard pierced her shoulder with a cold, stabbing pain.

She stretched upright, arching her back as if that could somehow diffuse the hurt. She glanced to her shoulder. The dress was untouched, but refocusing to the Hell, she saw her soul run through with The Scyon's icy spirit. It flowed through, mingling with her life threads. Suddenly, the gray-green thread shot from her, bringing out a bit of her golden being with it. As it pulled from her, a memory inflamed her mind. It was so real, she could smell the scent of winter on her brother as he walked, stony-faced, into the house four days after their father died. He didn't ask what happened. He didn't look at her. He just went to the table, sat down, and asked what was for dinner. Rage rose in her. She grasped the coffeepot. Her hand holding it trembled with all the hatred she felt toward him.

"Get out of my house," Allasan said.

As in her memory, Arvana drew her hand to her shoulder to throw.

"Ari!" Nan shouted.

No, it was the relic in Arvana's hand, not the coffeepot handle. It was The Scyon, not Allasan before her.

Nan was again charging it with Assaea. He was within striking distance.

The Scyon reared and the Beckoner went white. This time it wasn't afraid, didn't flinch.

Nan thrust Assaea straight upward into the Beckoner. It made a flat, cracking sound, and Nan stood as if transfixed. His hair eerily floated out from his head.

Assaea glowed brighter in this world than it did in Hell. The bolt of light connecting Nan and The Scyon abruptly stopped and Nan's hair fell limp, then so did the rest of his body and he slumped to the ground.

Disbelief froze Arvana. It seemed an eternity before a realization broke the shell of shock: though Nan didn't move, he still glowed with life and his hand still gripped the sword.

"You spent your sword to destroy what does not matter." The Scyon's lipless mouth sneered at Nan. The Beckoner's case was broken. Inside were a green plate and a tangle of wires that popped and fizzled. White, bitter-smelling smoke drifted from it. "I don't need the Beckoner. I have escaped death." It raised a claw to score Nan's motionless body.

Without thought, Arvana launched herself between them and hitting The Scyon's arm, deflected the claw from Nan. The Blue Eye popped from her hand and landed faceup in the snow. As she reached for it, The Scyon swept her to it as easily as if she were a small child. It clutched her to its chest, pressing Arvana's face to the stinking hole where the Beckoner used to be.

The air stirred wildly, whipping the snow into a storm. Arvana's feet lifted from the ground. She pressed away from The Scyon until there was a small space between their bodies through which she could see the ground. There was Nan, his hand kneading the snow. Life still glowed around him, but he was growing more distant and so was the Blue Eye's light. The Scyon was rising to the opening in the atrium. Soon she would be beyond helping Nan. She had been so close to defeating The Scyon, but had let it fight her with her own weaknesses—weaknesses she'd endured.

This time The Scyon wouldn't escape her. She looked to the Blue Eye.

The beast's icy-green spirit spun downward to the relic.

As The Scyon's spirit whooshed through the relic, its bodily wings slowed. It struggled to stay at the opening in the atrium roof. In Hell, Arvana watched The Scyon's spirit emerge from the Blue Eye. It jetted upward. The foremost part of it took the form of a coyote's head.

Teeth bared, the coyote hurled toward them. It circled behind The Scyon, and she lost sight of it.

Pain punctured Arvana's thigh. The coyote had come up behind her and gnashed her exposed upper thigh. With a wrench of its jaws, it ripped a deep gouge in her spirit, releasing in a flood all the regret she felt over her father. Engulfed by it, she forgot about The Scyon. The coyote dissolved into a green vapor, and then a barrage of feelings, but no vision, registered with her mind.

She should never have desired Payter, never gone on the sleigh ride. Maker, why hadn't it been her instead of her father? She could have seen it coming and escaped. The rest of her life she would have spent at home with her father. They would have been happy. She'd never have gone to Solace. At this moment, the Solacians would be kneeling for evening prayer. Chane would be carrying his boys on his shoulders. Nan would be wearing his fine general's coat.

Layered over the regret was the thought that at last, this was her penance. Everything would be changed. She could be happy now. The terrible hurt would stop. But it didn't. The wound throbbed. Each pulse ebbed with regret.

Even if she could relive *that* day, staying home instead of sledding, it wouldn't fix anything. Though Arvana saw the spirit coyote coming, she was unable to escape it. The mad coyote would have killed her. What joy would her father have had at burying her? If she had evaded the mad coyote, how happy would she have been living with her father? She had desired Payter. Soon or later, she would have felt that desire again and would have become bitter at her duty to remain home.

Even her guilt wasn't a pure thing.

The Scyon's grasp around her loosened.

Yes, drop her. End this. Nothing else had ended it.

The teetering sensation of being barely suspended in the air stunned Arvana from the pain of the guilt. She looked down from the dizzying height. Through snow clouds whipped up by The Scyon's beating wings, she saw Nan lying in the snow. Dear Nan. How near she had come to forsaking him to nurse the worthless grief in her soul. She wouldn't leave him to The Scyon.

She bent forward, threw her arms around The Scyon's neck, and then craned to see the ground. The Blue Eye was a small glowing spot in the snow. She fixed her gaze on the relic and her heart on The Scyon's soul.

"Go to Hell," she cried.

The Blue Eye sucked a torrent of green vapor.

The Scyon screeched.

The Blue Eye stopped glowing.

A fierce wind gathered up The Scyon's spirit in its vortex and tore through Hell. Arvana closed her eyes to break her connection with the Blue Eye. The warmth of life bloomed within her, but still she felt the rush of wind. Was she still in Hell?

She opened her eyes. The Scyon's body was twisted around hers.

They weren't in Hell.

They were falling.

HOLLOW VICTORY

The forward lob of his head jerked Degarius to his senses. He was being hauled up by his arms. Instinctively, he tightened his grip on his sword.

Gherians.

Where was Ari? At a stand, he spit snow from his lips and said in Gherian, "Let me go, you bastards," and to his surprise, they released him.

The Scyon's body was lying on its back in a broken heap in the middle of the floor. A bearish Gherian soldier with a full red beard and a commander's peacock feather in his hat was heaving off one of the creature's wings that was folded over its corpse. The wing fell with a dead *thump* into the snow and glass.

Ari was atop the creature, still embraced by The Scyon's sinewy arms. The commander walked over the wing, peeled The Scyon's arms from her, and helped her to her feet.

Degarius's head went fuzzy with relief and trying to make sense of it. For all love, his Ari must have killed The Scyon with the Blue Eye. She looked shaken but was alive. Joy welled in him until he noted the dozen men standing behind the overturned table that had been inside the pavilion. Half of the men were clerics or generals, the other half Fortress Guards with their swords drawn—except one. His right coat sleeve was empty, pinned across the front of his general's coat, as if his hand was to his heart. He looked vaguely familiar.

"Execute them," said the young man with one arm.

Ari had to use the Blue Eye. Degarius squinted. It wasn't in her hands. Damn it all. What was a sword against a dozen men? Telling himself he had to go down fighting, he raised his blade, but then felt one at his back and heard a Gherian tell him not to move.

As Degarius stiffened at the sensation of the blade at his back, the Fortress Guards thrust their swords into what looked to be two generals and four clerics. The big Gherian commander with Ari had wrapped his thick arms around her and turned her away from the brutality.

The young man who'd given the execution order didn't bother to watch. He went to The Scyon's corpse and twisted the sovereign's ring from its claw of a finger. The rule of Gheria was now open for the taking, and this young man was making his claim, evidently with the backing of the Fortress Guards. One-handed, he worked the ring upon his finger and held his hand aloft. The Guards raised their bloody swords in tribute and cried, "Sovereign Sibelian."

Sibelian. He was Alenius's adopted son and heir.

"Move the beast," Sibelian shouted. "I want to find it."

The soldiers gathered around the corpse and between pulling the wing and pushing the shoulders, rolled the body. They fell to their knees and combed through snow until one rose and presented Sibelian with something metal. The Blue Eye.

Sibelian, turning the relic over in his fingers, approached Degarius. Its cover was bent back and the lens broken. Inside was a cracked green plate covered with silver wires and odd small silver dots. To one of the generals he said, "Rorke never came. Go find him and tell him his generals are dead and his Blue Eye destroyed. Then kill him." He slipped the broken relic into the pocket of his fur coat, then drew his sword and raised it to Degarius's chin. "Looks familiar, doesn't it Stellansonson."

How did Sibelian know who he was? Degarius looked down his nose at the sword. It was his captain's sword. "Where did you get it?"

"Lake Sandela. You must have lost it there, after you cut off my arm."

Degarius began to shake his head, but Sibelian added, "It was at Two Days Gorge."

He was a dead man.

"Perhaps you didn't know that Alenius sent his son to stop you."

"I didn't know."

"And would that have stopped your blade, had you known."

"No."

Sibelian laughed and lowered the sword point to Degarius's neck. "Then why should I spare you?"

Spare him? It dawned on Degarius that if Sibelian didn't execute him, the coup might save more than their lives. Sibelian wasn't Alenius's blood son, and the general in charge of the army on the front was Alenius's brother. Sibelian's claim to the throne was by no means settled, especially if Alenius's brother won a great battle against Sarapost and swayed the military to his side; several other generals were sure to side with the brother. "If you kill us, enjoy wearing the sovereign's ring. It won't be on your finger for long."

"What do you mean?" Sibelian drew his shoulders back as if he was already adjusting the mantle of his power.

"While in Acadia, I negotiated the treaty securing troops for the campaign. Acadia is entitled to territory as well as spoils. If our alliance wins, Sarapost could be surrounded by Acadian-held lands, and with an Acadian queen, our independence might not last with a half-Acadian heir. A victory over the Gherians would be bittersweet for Sarapost. We would rather not fight this war. Some of your generals share the sentiment. They don't want to lose their tenants to promises of free Sarapostan land. Do you want to fight when your time might now be better spent securing the loyalty of your generals?" Degarius nodded to the bodies of the generals who had already been executed.

"But how am I to trust you that Sarapost doesn't wish this fight? What reassurance do I have that what you propose isn't a trick to lure me into killing the generals? With our army distracted with the question of allegiance, Sarapost would gain an advantage and attack. What authority do you have to negotiate treaties?"

"I came without Sarapost's sanction or knowledge. Prince Fassal, however, is my friend. If you guarantee our safe passage through Gheria, you have my word the war will be called off."

"I heard you are wanted, Stellansonson, by the Acadians for the murder of Lerouge. Should I trust a murderer? How good can your word be?"

With a glance to the dead clerics and generals, Degarius said, "As good as yours, but I will give you more than my word if you promise me, too, that no harm will come to her." He nodded to Ari and then held out his sword. "Do you know what it is?"

"Assaea. I could have killed you for it."

"I know. It's why I thought I might trust you."

Sibelian regarded Degarius through narrowed, astute eyes. "Standing orders are to begin battle tomorrow at sunrise."

"If we ride all night—" Degarius began.

"If I ride all night, I may be able to take care of the generals," Sibelian finished.

Degarius knew what Sibelian meant by "take care of"—he would kill the generals before the border troops learned of Alenius's death.

One of the guards who had acted as executioner asked permission to speak. "If we took Megreth's head, if they thought you killed it after it turned on Alenius and the clerics, the army would be yours."

Sibelian frowned in disgust. "I will not claim false laurels. Stellansonson and his lady did it."

Degarius saw the brilliance of the plan. It could save thousands of lives, maybe even their own. "An honor is not an honor if thousands needlessly die for it to be known. We ask you to abide your guard's suggestion. We will testify to Sarapost it was the case."

On a long exhale, Sibelian considered. Then, his mouth crept into a smile. He gave Degarius his captain's sword and then took Assaea.

Degarius didn't notice the sensation of the sword leaving his hand. It wasn't what made him complete, wasn't the better half of him.

"Release Stellansonson. He will ride with me to the border." He weighed Assaea in his hand. "I was promised this sword and believe me, I wanted it, wanted anything I might eventually be able to use to stop this madness. I was there when Alenius had the Beckoner sewn into his chest." Sibelian threw a repulsed look at The Scyon's corpse. "I wished I could have killed him then, but the eunuchs were on their guard. I know what he became. Now, I must thank my enemies for delivering Gheria from a madman. Who is the lady? Is she the Solacian?"

The Gherian commander escorted Ari to Sibelian. Without a coat, she was shivering.

"The lady is Miss Nazar," Degarius said.

"I would take your hand and kiss it, but you see I only have one. Know I would not, will not, hurt you. I am a man of my word." He raised Assaea as in salute. "Captain Berlson, you bring Miss Nazar."

The commander removed his coat and draped it over Ari's shoulders, put his hat on her head, then went down on one knee and told her that his name was Berlson, that he had seen everything and regretted he had not helped her until the end. He would allow no woman's valor to be greater than his own. He would lay down his life for her for saving Gheria. Ari, who obviously didn't understand half of what Berlson was saying, looked anxious for him to rise.

"You have an admirer," Degarius said. For once, he was glad of it.

❦

The snow-sputtering sky made the night black. With an escort of torch-bearing Fortress Guards, the small circle of light in which they rode moved as fast as was possible down the snowy Gherian roads. A sleigh carried the fire draeden's head. As Degarius rode, he recalled all he knew of his father's profession. His fear was the parties would meet and opportunism would sink his intentions. How was one to prevent that?

First, he must know with whom he was dealing, which was more difficult than he expected. As well as he knew Fassal, he could not absolutely say that the prince would subscribe to his peace plan. Though Fassal had seen the brutality of war, he was still an excitable youth. Would he decide to launch the campaign against the Gherians now that uncertain leadership weakened them? Would he risk Acadia gaining contiguous territory to Sarapost in exchange for the security of defeating the Gherians, their longtime enemy? On the other hand, would he take a chance on peace with a potentially unstable neighbor? If Sibelian secured enough troops, he could decide to attack Sarapost to prove his power. Was Sibelian going to be a trustworthy negotiator? Often, one tyrant replaced another in a coup.

Peace. At one time, Degarius would have spoken passionately for war, to decimate the Gherians in their time of weakness. Repay them for their trespasses. Why did he want peace now? *Have I become my father?* The twinge of amusement lasted a second. He wanted peace for the girls whose tattered frocks smelled of tears and dirty soldiers. He wanted peace for the boys and men, black coat or blue, so their lives wouldn't end with their bodies crumpled in inhuman positions, their faces locked in inhuman expressions. But not Alenius's kind of peace, the kind of peace that came from fear instead of men making choices by the governance of their hearts. Degarius grimaced at the benevolent picture he was painting of himself and how Heran Kieran would approve his rationale. He just wanted to sit at his table at Fern Clyffe again— under different circumstances.

Finally, they paused to rest the horses and warm themselves. Arvana, huddled in Commander Berlson's huge coat, was worried about the effect of prolonged cold on the fragile skin of Nan's feet. Yet she kept the concerns private. He was sitting across the fire with Sibelian, and she wouldn't embarrass him with her womanly anxiety.

Berlson, Arvana's self-appointed protector, pointed to Degarius and spoke to her in slow Gherian so she would understand. "Stellansonson husband?"

"Nan..." No, she mustn't call him that aloud. Perhaps in the trials of battle it had not mattered when she called him *Nan*, but now was different. "Degarius...Stellansonson...is not husband." She felt the lump of the emerald ring inside the mittens Berlson had given her; she'd left Lina's fine gloves in the pocket of the coat she gave to the Lily Girl. She couldn't keep the ring or sell it. Nan had his reason for giving it to her. It wasn't a gift. It was a payment she'd neither asked for nor wanted. It was her right to return it. If she could just rid herself of every worldly reminder of him, she could start a true life anew—the life she never started in Solace because she'd kept her father's kithara. "I was a Solacian, but now want to go to Sylvania. If I had coin I would make a home there..."

"Coin? You need coin for home?" Berlson rose, circled the fire to Sibelian, and after a word with him, took something. He returned to Arvana and sat again beside her. "From Sibelian," he said and presented two gold pieces the size of her palm.

"Too much." She tried to give one back.

Berlson shook his head adamantly. "Sibelian once promised you home and hearth. He is good to his word."

"Promised me?"

"Yes." Berlson smiled so wide the corners of his mouth disappeared into his bushy beard.

"I don't understand—"

"No, you can't understand." Berlson took her mittened hand and curled it over the coins.

She could not estimate their worth with any exactness, but knew they would purchase far more than a home. She pictured a new kithara. "Kithara," she said to Berlson and wanted to tell him about rosewood and inlay. However, her Gherian did not extend to these rarer words so she removed her mittens, put the coins in the coat pocket, and pantomimed playing.

❈ ❈ ❈

Before sunrise, they arrived in the territory where the two armies camped. Degarius went along to witness Sibelian rouse from bed the generals sympathetic to the coup and to execute Alenius's brother and supporters. Degarius heard every order. Sibelian was clear in his directives—no engagement with the Sarapostans. The troops marveled at the draeden's head and whispered in admiration of Sibelian's deed.

In preparation for their venture into Sarapostan lands, the Gherian standard was rigged with a white parlay cloth. As they started, the snow thickened but a Gherian scout who knew the land intimately was leading them to the Sarapostan encampment. They slowed to cross the small stream that would become the Odis River. While regaining speed, a group of horsemen shot out from a windbreak on their left. Because of the snow and dark, Degarius could hear the familiar mix of horses and men, but could not see the force until they were on top of them with drawn weapons. Evidently, the Sarapostans could not see the white pennant. Degarius bellowed for his countrymen to stand down, but they were already engaging the Fortress Guards and couldn't hear him over the battle cries.

⚜ ⚜ ⚜

"Stay with me," Commander Berlson shouted to Arvana, and she pulled her horse in next to his. They were trying to ride out of the melee. A Sarapostan with a ready sword appeared beside Berlson. The captain laid a huge blow on the man, knocking the sword from him, and he dropped a horse length back. Then, the Sarapostan was at Arvana's right. He brought his horse flush against hers. Their stirrups met. She felt a sharp thrust to her side, then the Sarapostan split from her.

At last the words "envoy, envoy" were universally shouted by Sarapostans and Gherians. Several of the Sarapostans recognized Degarius, and they vied to ride at his side as escorts into camp.

Arvana wondered why her side should hurt so dreadfully where the Sarapostan had hit her. The horse's movement and her respiration exacerbated the pain. However, the horizon was alight with Sarapostan campfires so she gritted her teeth; the end was near. They rode through rows of tents and lanes of slushy snow to a village, then to a house, its windows golden with candlelight. Prince Fassal and his huge dog burst out. Nan dismounted while his horse was still walking. He and Fassal embraced into a single silhouette against a rectangle of light spreading out from the house's open door. Their deep chortled laughter of greeting carried above the braying horses, shouting soldiers, and the dog's eager barking. Nan affectionately rubbed the dog's scruff. How free he was with them. Nan, Degarius, had never embraced her without it ending in reservation or regret. She knew she should be happy for him. He had averted a war. They had stopped a terrible evil. Still, it made her sad to know that the joy was between Degarius and Fassal. Hers was always to be a private one. *Oh, Ari.* The sadness dissolved into an amorphous feeling of fatigue. She knew she should dismount, but she didn't have the strength to lift her leg. How long had it been since she'd slept or eaten? It seemed like weeks. Her side had hurt so much, but now it didn't hurt at all. A low buzzing closed in around her head. Vaguely, she felt the reins slip from her mittens.

❖—❖—❖

"What a dog you are, Degarius. I'm so damn glad to see you alive." Fassal wrung Degarius's hand. "Of all things, sneaking into Gheria in the midst of a coup."

"Speaking of dogs, call your beast off of me." Degarius laughed. Caspar kept jumping at his side.

One of Fassal's assistants took the dog's collar.

"Come, let me introduce you to Sovereign Sibelian," Degarius said. "I gave my word we'd call off the war."

Fassal and Sibelian had just exchanged bows when an urgent hail went up. "Degheria, Degheria. Stellansonson." It was Commander Berlson. Degarius turned around. Something was going on behind them. Riders were about-facing their horses.

"Go," Sibelian said.

Degarius, followed by Fassal and Sibelian, wove through the mingling Sarapostans and Gherians to a circle of men who'd dismounted. Those with lanterns held them aloft to illuminate whatever was in their midst. Degarius pushed through.

Berlson, his ruddy, fleshy face knotted, was crouching beside Ari. She was lying motionless in the snow. Blood stained the inside of her opened coat and her dress at the hip. "I didn't know,"

Berlson said. "They thought her a soldier...wearing my coat and hat."

For a long moment, Degarius just stood trying to understand the blurry image he saw. A part of him refused to believe it. Another part had seen this far too often. Both, as always, told him to stay back from it. Grief gutted you. He looked away, had to look at *anything* else. He blinked his eyes open as wide as they'd go and looked at the soldier bearing the Sarapostan standard. *Damn it, I'm a soldier.*

But then a hand lighted on his shoulder and Fassal muttered, "Oh brother," and it was as if Degarius's own weight was an unbearable force pulling him down. His knees buckled, and he came to them. He couldn't breathe. He bowed his head, and as he came over her and cradled her limp body to his, he exhaled the prayer that filled his chest to bursting. "Maker, don't take her. I beg you, don't take her."

Someone was pulling at Degarius's coat, as if trying to drag him away. "No," he growled. "You can't take her."

"Brother, my physician is here. You must let him tend her."

SOLACE

Field Marshall Fassal's house, Sarapost-Gheria battlefront

"Hera, you're awake! I was hoping you'd wake while I was here. You've slept the day."

"Princess Lerouge?" Arvana rubbed her knuckles to her eyes.

"Not Lerouge. Haven't you heard? I'm married."

Arvana began to prop herself on her elbows to survey her surroundings, but the motion ignited the pain in her side. The last thing she remembered was a blur of people around her, someone tugging at her clothes, and then a bitter taste in her mouth. Now she lay in a comfortable bed in a cozy room with a splendid fire and the princess bedside in a chair. "Are we in Sarapost?"

"Sarapost? We're at the front. It's much more diverting here than in Sarapost. I go among the soldiers every day and it cheers them. Evenings I host receptions for the officers. A Gherian officer is sitting outside your door and every so often, he looks in. I can't understand a word he says."

"Commander Berlson?"

"Does he look like a red-haired bear?"

"Has peace been made?"

"They are finalizing an agreement now." A crease marred Jesquin's brow. "I wished to be with you before, but I couldn't countenance being in the same room with the man who killed my brother. Gregory finally insisted he spare five minutes to witness the signing and took him downstairs."

"He was here?"

"It must have been terrible to be his captive all these months." Jesquin shuddered. "Gregory is so obstinately attached to him he refuses to see his character and give him to Acadia for trial."

"He did a great deed to help Sarapost." Arvana wanted to say that he sacrificed the thing dearest to him, his sword, for Sarapost, but it was all to be a secret.

"My husband said something to that effect—that he ventured to the Forbidden Fortress to negotiate the peace, but I can't agree with Gregory he deserves a generalship or a position in court for it. He's a murderer. By pure luck, he arrived after the coup. Did you see the beast? Gregory said they've brought its head, but he wouldn't let me see it. He says it is the most horrible thing ever and I'd have nightmares from it. Did you see Sibelian kill it?"

"Sibelian? Yes."

"He sounds ever so heroic. His men have fashioned him into a legend, like Lukis or Paulus. Perhaps all the clans will support him and...ah." The princess pivoted in her chair to lean over and right a bit of lace turned inward on Arvana's neckline. "It's one of my nightgowns. Do you like it? It's a bit plain, so I've never worn it, but it suits you. Don't worry if your stitches soil it a bit. I have many others."

Arvana noted for the first time the silky, white sleeves. She felt her side. A thick wad of bandages covered her hip.

"I have a grand idea. I've been thinking on it while you slept. Since Solace is no more, you could start a new order here in Sarapost. I would make a generous donation."

Start a new order like the Founder? The idea of it made Arvana ease back into the pillow. Being a Solacian was a worthy life to which she was accustomed. It would be a comfort to go back to it, even with the challenges of organizing a new order. But at the thought of a narrow cot, her body ached for the warmth of his body curled to hers in the Gherian inn's bed. How could she ask novices to forsake earthly desires when she could not? "It's a kind offer, but I renounced my profession. Sibelian gave me a handsome gift. I shall go to Sylvania."

"You cannot!" Jesquin pouted and testily crossed her arms.

"The last thing I would want is to disappoint you, but I can't stay in Sarapost." Arvana ran her thumb against the smooth back of his ring. "I know you understand."

"It's because of *him*, isn't it? Oh, what a relief that is. Gregory bet me a week's pocket money the horrid man turned down the generalship so you would go with him to his country house. I knew—"

Arvana rose to sitting despite the pain and tightness at her hip. "He declined the generalship?"

"You must lie back down. Gregory's physician had to stitch your side. He said you were immensely lucky the way the blade entered and that you were wearing that heavy coat, riding breeches, and a dress."

"He's downstairs?" Arvana threw back the covers and shifted her feet from the bed. Jesquin jumped up. Her alarmed expression swam in Arvana's still-woozy head. She steadied herself on the bedpost. "Where's my dress?"

"It's quite ruined, I imagine."

An extra blanket was across the foot of the bed. Arvana unfolded it and eased it over her shoulders like a cape.

"Please get back in bed."

"Berlson," Arvana called. The door opened, and in peered the commander. In Gherian, she asked, "Will you help me go...?" She didn't know the word for downstairs, so she pointed downward. "I want to speak with Degarius."

"I'll bring Stellansonson to you."

"Not in this room. I won't abide it," the princess said. "What he did—"

"Please take me, Berlson."

"For a moment," he said and gently put an arm around Arvana's shoulder. He assisted her down the steps to the parlor door just off the foyer. Without knocking, he opened the door. "Stellansonson."

Stares and the clinks of coffee cups settling into their saucers greeted them.

"I heard you rejected a generalship," Arvana said into the silence. "Is it true?"

Degarius, without his glasses, squinted, gulped the coffee in his mouth, frowned, and rose. "Excuse me."

"With pleasure," Prince Fassal said and to Arvana added, "You gave us quite the scare."

Degarius came straightaway. Berlson remained in the foyer with them, but stood to the side. It would be pointless to ask him to leave.

"You should be in bed," Degarius said. "Let me help you back."

"I slept enough. You haven't." Despite his ever-noble stature, his complexion was sallow. She looked to his boots. "It was cold during the ride. Did your feet suffer?"

"Let me help you back—"

"I came to ask, I heard...the generalship meant the world to you. Why won't you have it? Is it because of the peace?"

"The peace? Yes. I think I've earned the right to go home."

"Home." There was the answer. Fassal, as she, had speculated too far into his reasons for declining the generalship. It was only out of gentlemanly courtesy he sat with her when she slept, just as he'd done when Kieran was ill. Nan had been through much and simply wished to have no more of soldiering or politics. Ferne Clyffe was the dream he'd been deferring. She thought of her own recent dream—the house in Sylvania, the kithara—and reminded herself of the pleasures of being one's own mistress. "Yes, this is all over now. I wish to go home, too. Sylvania is beautiful in spring."

"Sylvania?"

"By Sibelian's generosity, I will have my own place. And..." Arvana twisted his ring off and held it to him. It was *all* over. "Forgive me for losing the necklace. Please keep this. I know it's special to your family. We've been through much together. It's my way of thanking you." He kept his hands to his sides. Why must he make this more difficult than it was? She raised her gaze to his face to plead with him, but his eyes were hard.

"It isn't your way of thanking me," he said.

"I...you can't understand...I can't keep it. It would be cruel of you to insist."

"No, I understand." He reached out and took the ring.

Dear Maker, why did she want to cry? Everything between them was finally untangled, and she had freed herself of the one material thing that bound them together. But it wasn't as the Solacians taught. Things didn't bind her heart. Wiping her eyes, the blanket slipped from her shoulders and a cold draft wafted around her. She began to bend to retrieve the blanket, but her side stung and in her moment of hesitation, he was already retrieving it. He wrapped it around her. Taking the edges, she clutched them in her fists over her chest and then clenched her eyes shut to keep further tears in check, but a hot stream rolled down one side of her face. "I want to go upstairs, Captain Berlson."

"I'll take you upstairs. And if you truly want to go to Sylvania, I shall deliver you there myself. But, Ari..." At the sensation of his finger tracing the wet path along her cheek, she opened her eyes. "Forgive me if your pain gives me hope I don't deserve. Your good heart loved me once and mine has always been yours. Yes, it's true. Well, perhaps not always. The first time I saw you, I confess I noted that you were beautiful, but I put it out of mind and thought only of my sword. But the second time, in Lady Martise's garden, you told me our professions weren't so different, that I was good and the Maker had a special grace for me. You can't know what those words have meant to me...coming from *you*. Every day since then, you have been in my thoughts, and so often, they have been a trial. I denied what I felt—at first with good reason. I had to respect who you were. The rest...you don't know what a torment my behavior has been to me...and all to a woman whose greatest fault was thinking me good."

"You lost your generalship. It was what you wanted."

"It was what I *thought* I wanted. At Ferne Clyffe, I understood my error, but with going north...no man with a shred of honor could ask the woman he loves to undertake such a mission. And my courage has always been of a particular kind. I could always tell myself I had nothing to lose. It made me fearless. The night at the inn, after what you shared with me, I only let you in the coach by telling myself you must regret it, regret me. But the odd thing is, when we were in the Fortress garden, when I knew what the Gherians would do to you, I fought harder than I ever have. I wish I wouldn't have had to learn the truth of my courage that way. I wish this could have all been *different*. Ari, look at me. Tell me you understand."

Through the bleary film of tears, Arvana saw the tenderness in his eyes. They were the blue of the great, vast sky that lay in a warm embrace over the fields.

"Can you only imagine yourself as a general's wife? I hoped you would prefer...I would prefer..."

From the open parlor door, Fassal's dog loped toward them until his leash, at its length, jerked him to a standstill. Behind Fassal stood all the Gherian and Sarapostan dignitaries. "Caspar, not now." Fassal, in the doorway, reeled back the dog. "Well brother, what is your fate? I pray you've saved me a week's worth of pocket money."

Degarius held the ring poised between two fingers. "Forgive me how I gave this to you the first time...though my sentiment was..."

Laughing and crying all at once, Arvana extended her hand. "Oh, Nan." He slipped the ring on her finger and rising on her tiptoes, she kissed him freely, joyously. The blanket dropped from her shoulders again, but this time, Nan wrapped his arms around her, drew her to his heat, to the galloping of his heart, to the warm, comforting smell of his body. If her small human love could be so abundant, how much more was the Maker's?

"Dear Maker," she whispered.
"Yes," Nan said.

EPILOGUE

23rd of Summer, Year 740 of the Saviors

Dearest Jesquin,
    I hope my letter finds you in tolerable spirits at the Citadel. I am much relieved to hear that our nephew has regained his sense after the brutal throw from his horse.

My talks at the Forbidden Fortress with Sibelian are finished. I'm sensible of the honor of my delegation being the first non-Gherians admitted and tentatively will call our meeting a success. We reached agreement on possession of nearly all of the disputed borderland territory. But I doubt how long Sibelian's rule will stand. Alenius's blood kin are drumming support from those who expected generous plots of Sarapostan land and from those who protest against the abolishment of the cabinet, Lily Girls, and making of eunuchs. What loathsome neighbors we shall have again if the alliance against him prevails.

Now, for happier news. I'm writing you from the sweet home of your tutor and shall stay another night before returning to Sarapost. Ferne Clyffe is a vast place and Caspar has enjoyed the run of it. The ingrate would probably not think of me once if I left him here.

I found your tutor exceedingly well settled and in glowing health. She seems born to be the lady of a country estate—not just by tending a kitchen garden and playing her instrument for the occasional guest but also by keeping the accounts for both a home and a vast landholding. She is with her second child and hopes to welcome it within the moon. The first child, a girl who shall be three this autumn, is the image of her mother. She is a shy thing, hiding behind her father until he pulled her around, sat his straw hat upon her head, and rode her on his knee until she laughed. I know you can never love him as I do, but even you would have smiled to see the severe captain neighing and thumping his heel. Perhaps it will make you a little easier of your tutor's fate to know he gives her and their child the same unswerving devotion he gave Sarapost as a captain, however here to a happier end. But I shall say no more on this. I only thought you'd wish to know your tutor is well.

As to your last note, certainly a grand dance to mark the harvest is a fine idea. I leave the details in your capable hands.

Give your father my best wishes for his birthday,

Gregory

THE END

ABOUT THE AUTHOR

With her ever-patient family, the impatient Anna Steffl lives in Athens, Georgia, home of the New World gods of football and alternative music. She has held a string of wildly unrelated jobs, from frying chicken to one that required applying for a Department of Defense security clearance.

Find Anna at:

Website: www.annasteffl.com

Facebook: www.facebook.com/annasteffl

Twitter: @AnnaKurtzSteffl